Love Lessons

GINA WILKINS

MILLS & BOON®

First published in Great Britain 2007
Large Print edition 2007
Silhouette Books Limited, Eton House,
18-24 Paradise Road, Richmond, Surrey, TW9 1SR

© Gina Wilkins 2006

ISBN-13: 978 0 263 19861 4

Set in Times Roman 16¾ on 20¾ pt.
35-0607-62886

Printed and bound in Great Britain
by Antony Rowe Ltd, Chippenham, Wiltshire

GINA WILKINS

is a bestselling and award-winning author who has written more than seventy books for Harlequin and Silhouette. She credits her successful career in romance to her long, happy marriage and her three "extraordinary" children.

A lifelong resident of central Arkansas, Ms. Wilkins sold her first book to Harlequin in 1987 and has been writing full-time since. She has appeared on the Waldenbooks, B. Dalton and *USA TODAY* bestseller lists. She is a three-time recipient of the Maggie Award for Excellence sponsored by Georgia Romance Writers, and has won several awards from the reviewers of *Romantic Times BOOKreviews*.

With thanks to my two scientist
daughters for their input and to
my son for his sample AP biology tests.
They got their math and science skills
from their dad!

Chapter One

Norman, the sleek, black-and-white cat, sat expectantly on the kitchen table across from Catherine Travis's chair. Her mother would be horrified to see a cat on the table, but Catherine merely shrugged in response to that thought. Her parents were in China, enjoying each other's company, while she was stuck here alone in Little Rock, Arkansas. Since Norman was the only one available on this September Sunday evening to help Catherine celebrate her thirtieth birthday, he could pretty much sit anywhere he liked, as far as she was concerned.

He watched intently as she lit the single candle topping a chocolate-frosted cupcake. She sat back to admire the flickering flame, noting the way it reflected in Norman's big, golden eyes. She couldn't help but smile at his expression as he looked from her to the candle and then back again.

"You look as though you know exactly what we're doing," she remarked to the nine-month-old cat who had made his home with her for the past six months. "I half expect you to start singing the happy birthday song to me now."

Norman meowed obligingly. The sound was actually rather musical, Catherine decided. "Thank you. That was lovely."

She leaned forward to blow out the candle but then stopped herself. "Oh, wait. If I'm going to throw myself a birthday party, I should do it right. I'm supposed to make a wish before I blow out the candle, aren't I?"

Norman's ears flicked in interest. Curling his tail around his white feet, he sat up straighter, looking at her encouragingly. Although she knew darned well that he was waiting for the cat treat she was holding for him, she indulged herself with the pretense that he was actually interested in what she had to say.

"Okay, here's my wish. I wish I had someone with whom to share occasions like this. Birthdays, holidays, other special events. As much as I appreciate your companionship, Normie, it would be nice to have a *human* male in my life."

She blew out the candle. She and Norman both watched the thin line of white smoke drift from the blackened wick to dissipate above the table. Only then did she set the salmon-flavored treat in front of her cat. "There you go, pal. Enjoy."

He sniffed at the treat, took an experimental lick, then began to nibble delicately, his tail twitching with pleasure. Catherine peeled the paper from the sides of the cupcake and took a bite, letting the rich chocolate frosting dissolve slowly on her tongue. "Mmm. Good."

Norman responded with a muted, whirring noise that might have been agreement.

She reached out to stroke his silky back, and

he arched into her touch. If only people were as easy to understand as her cat, she mused wistfully. Men, especially.

She had a couple of advanced degrees, was quite successful in her career as a biomedical researcher, had a few good friends and a nice apartment, but she had never really learned the art of dating. As far as she knew, there were no classes in flirtation, and she had never picked up the talent in her science labs.

She had been focused so single-mindedly on her education and her career that she had missed out on learning how to play. She just wasn't a "fun" person, she thought with a sigh. The only men who had asked her out during the past couple of years had bored her half-senseless. She seemed destined to be alone with her work and her cat.

To distract herself from her mounting self-pity, she reached for the small stack of presents she had saved to open all at once. Her friend Karen Kupperman from work had given her a tin of herbal tea and a scented candle in a pretty cobalt glass holder. Practical and yet slightly self-indulgent—just the sort of gift Karen would appreciate herself.

Karen was in Europe now, on a two-week trip with her husband, Wayne. They had combined a vacation with a science conference in Geneva, and Karen had been looking forward to the excursion for months.

Catherine's other friend, Julia, a public attorney, had given her another practical, but elegant, present—a pair of soft brown leather gloves lined with cashmere. Lovely, she thought, trying them on to admire the perfect fit. Typical of Julia—who was currently in New York City at a convention of lawyers.

A couple of Catherine's graduate students had gone in together to buy her an emerald-green cashmere scarf. Rubbing it against her cheek, she murmured her appreciation of the luxuriously soft feel. She would enjoy this when the weather turned cold. Since it was almost the end of September now, it wouldn't be much longer until the temperatures began to drop.

Finally there was the package from her parents, both academics currently teaching at a university in China. They had sent her a beautiful silk blouse and a check. The blouse pleased her; the check made her frown.

She wished she could convince them that she was doing fine financially. An only child born to them rather late in life, she had been overprotected and indulged, gently pushed to follow in their academic footsteps, raised in a sheltered, Ivy-League environment that hadn't exactly prepared her for modern dating and socializing. And now, despite her career and her friends and her financial security—she was lonely on her birthday.

Biting her lip, she set the gifts aside and picked up her pet, snuggling into his neck. His purr vibrated against her cheek as she murmured, "I know wishes don't really come true, Norman, but just this once I'll try to believe...."

The day after Catherine's birthday was a Monday, and it started out with a minor frustration. After she had showered and dressed for work, she walked into the kitchen to prepare her breakfast, only to find one of the knobs from her stove broken off and lying on the linoleum floor.

"Great," she muttered, bending to pick it up. The knob had been loose for weeks—something she had meant to report but kept forgetting. She couldn't imagine how it had broken off by itself during the night, but here it was.

Shaking her head, she stepped over the cat winding himself around her ankles and picked up the phone to call the rental office. As it happened, the new maintenance guy had just stepped into the office, she was told, and he could come right then if it was convenient for her. It would take him only a couple of minutes to repair the knob.

She agreed, then called her lab to let them know she would be a little late. Fortunately, her schedule was flexible that day, so she didn't have to rush in. If something had to break, it seemed it had happened at a convenient time, she mused, walking toward the front door in anticipation of the maintenance man's arrival. While she was accustomed to prompt responses from the management of her upscale apartment complex, this was even faster than usual.

Three quick raps announced his arrival, and she opened her door. Then very nearly dropped her jaw.

The last maintenance man who had repaired something in her apartment had been sixtyish, beer-bellied, balding and borderline surly. This guy looked somewhere in his mid- to late-twenties, athletically built, handsome in a blond, blue-eyed way, and flashed a hundred white teeth in a melt-your-spine smile.

All semblance of her usual intelligence and composure leaked right out of her brain. "Er...uh..."

"I'm Mike Clancy," he said, tapping the ID badge he wore on the pocket of a blue denim work shirt. He held a toolbox in his left hand. "Lucille said you've got a broken knob on your stove?"

"Oh, yes. Of course." Moving awkwardly out

of the doorway, she motioned toward the kitchen. "It's in there."

Brilliant, she thought with a slight wince. Where else would the stove be? The bathroom?

But he merely nodded and walked into the living room, casting a quick glance around at her carefully put-together green, burgundy and cream decor. "I like the way you've decorated. It looks real comfortable."

"Thank you." Since comfort had been the primary criterion for each piece she had selected, she was pleased by the adjective.

"Well, hello." Mike bent to offer a friendly hand to Norman, who sniffed him, then promptly rolled onto his back in a shameless bid for a belly scratch. Chuckling, Mike obliged, generating a rumbling purr that Catherine could hear from where she stood.

"He likes you," she commented unnecessarily. "He usually hides from strangers."

"He can probably tell that I like cats. What's his name?"

Watching that capable-looking, nicely shaped

hand stroking the cat's fur, and unable to miss noticing how Mike's jeans strained against his crouching thighs, Catherine had to take a moment to come up with the answer. "Norman. His name is Norman."

"Hey, there, Norman." He scratched just under Norman's pointy black chin, causing the silly cat to go into a frenzy of purring and wriggling. And then he straightened, to the disappointment of both cat and owner. "Okay. Where's the knob?"

Doubting he would appreciate an audience while he worked, Catherine stayed in the living room, but the apartment just happened to be arranged so that she could see him from the couch, where she had settled with the newspaper. She read maybe three words of the lead story, and those only when he glanced her way. The rest of the time, she simply watched him from beneath her eyelashes, struck by the novelty of having such a good-looking man in her kitchen.

Norman wasn't nearly as circumspect in his staring. He sat in the kitchen doorway, ears perked and nose twitching as he watched Mike work. Occasionally he glanced at Catherine as if to say, "Why are you way over there when your visitor is in here?"

Or maybe she was just projecting.

It took only a few minutes for Mike to repair the stove. He came out of the kitchen all tousled hair and gleaming smile, and her breath caught hard in her throat. "It's fixed," he announced. "Anything else you need before I go?"

Maybe a woman who'd learned how to flirt would answer that leading question with a witty comeback. A funny innuendo that would make him laugh, then give her a second look.

Catherine said only, "No, that's all. Thank you for coming so promptly."

"You're welcome." With a last pat for Norman, Mike let himself out, telling her to call again if she needed any other repairs.

Catherine closed and locked the door behind him, then sagged against it. She wasn't usually the type to notice such things, but Mike Clancy had one fine, tight butt encased in those soft denim jeans. She wasn't sure whether to be more dismayed or relieved that she had noticed this time.

At least it proved she was still in the game, she finally decided—even if only as a quiet spectator.

Late Wednesday afternoon Mike tapped on the door of apartment 906. If no one was home, he was authorized to let himself in and handle the repair job he'd been assigned, but he heard someone stirring inside. He smiled when the attractive brunette who had let him in only a couple of days earlier opened the door to him again. "I understand you have a broken window blind."

Her cheeks were pink, her expression chagrined when she nodded. "I haven't needed maintenance in almost a year, and now I've had two problems in one week. I'm sorry to be so much trouble."

"That's what I'm here for." Had it been anyone else, he might have suspected ulterior motives. It wouldn't be the first time he'd been called to a woman's apartment on a trumped-up excuse. But he would bet this woman was different.

For one thing, Catherine Travis—*Dr.* Catherine Travis, he reminded himself, having been told a little about this tenant by the rather gossipy apartment office manager—seemed genuinely put out that she'd had to request his services again. For another—well, get real. This woman was class from her neat brown bob to her sensibly shod feet. Hardly the type to angle for a quick fling with the maintenance man.

In this case he could almost be disappointed, he thought.

The living room window she led him to gave her a view of the parking lot and the swimming pool on the other side of the compound. A sliding glass door on another wall of the living room led onto a small balcony shaded by a big oak tree, which grew right at the corner of her end apartment. The balcony, too, overlooked the parking lot, except for the little patch of grass and bushes that lined the sidewalk leading to her steps.

The view from the large, back bedroom was better, he knew, though he hadn't been into that particular room in this two-bedroom apartment. From there she would be able to see the Arkansas River beyond the levee that protected the complex from flooding.

Catherine motioned toward the crookedly hanging window blind, the gesture emphasizing the gracefulness he had noted about her before. Slender and just slightly above average in height, she looked as though she could have been a model or a glamorous actress, rather than the scientist he knew her to be.

Her face was a perfect oval, framed by glossy brown hair shot with golden highlights that looked natural. Her eyes were a dark chocolate brown, her nose small and straight, her lips softly curved. Even dressed in a casual red knit top and comfortable-looking black slacks with black flats, she had a sort of classic poise about her that he would bet his sisters would openly envy.

"I don't know what happened," she said, her voice low and rich. "When I tried to open the blinds this morning to let in some sunlight, they just broke in my hand."

"That happens sometimes," he said with a shrug. "Especially with these plastic brackets. I've brought another blind with me. It won't take but a few minutes to replace it."

She nodded. "Thank you."

Feeling something brushing against his leg, he glanced down and grinned. "Well, hello, Norman. Nice to see you again."

The cat meowed a greeting, then arched and purred when Mike reached down to stroke his soft fur.

"He seems to remember you," Catherine remarked, watching them. "You really do have a way with cats."

"I grew up with them. At one time my sisters had four in the house with us, one cat for each sister. I had a pet snake at the time, just as a way to assert my masculinity."

"You have four sisters?"

He chuckled and straightened away from her cat. "All older. There are a few people who might tell you I was just a bit spoiled growing up."

Her smile transformed her face in a way that

made his pulse jump in instinctive male reaction. It added warmth and personality to her cool expression and drew his attention again to her perfectly shaped lips. "I'm sure that's not true."

"Actually, it's absolutely true," he admitted with a laugh. "I was shamelessly indulged."

Whatever she might have said in response was interrupted by the ring of her telephone. Her smile vanished. "Excuse me," she said, and turned to pick up the cordless extension that had been lying on the glass-topped wood coffee table.

He concentrated on his work as she carried the phone into the kitchen. While Norman lay at his feet begging for attention, he unscrewed the broken blind from the window casing. He wasn't trying to eavesdrop on Catherine's conversation, but he couldn't help overhearing a few snatches of what she was saying. Not that it mattered. Though she was speaking English, she might as well have been talking in a foreign language.

Obviously, the caller was someone from her work. She seemed to be giving instructions to whoever it was on how to do some sort of procedure that apparently involved a lot of steps and many multisyllabic terms that Mike had never heard.

He'd been told that some men were intimidated by brainy women. He, on the other hand, had nothing but respect for intelligent women, having been raised in a house full of them.

As for himself, he was smart enough to read the signs when a woman was interested in him, and he wasn't getting any of those signals from Catherine Travis. So, despite his respect for her body *and* her brains, he would keep things strictly professional while he was here.

He glanced at the coffee table as he set the broken blind on the floor and reached for the new one he'd brought with him. A stack of science journals and notebooks teetered at one end of the table, looking as though she'd been reading through them when he'd arrived. A workaholic? Seemed to be in character with his first impressions of her.

By the time she had finished her call, he had just completed the installation of the new blind.

He opened and closed it a couple of times, raised and lowered the slats to assure himself that everything was working correctly, then he closed his toolbox. "All done," he said as Catherine came back into the room. "I told you it wouldn't take long."

She nodded. "I appreciate it. I'll tell Lucille how much I've appreciated your quick responses this week."

He shrugged. "It's been a pretty slow week. You seem to be one of the few tenants having breakdowns at the moment."

To his pleasure, the smile he had admired before returned. "I got lucky, I guess," she said.

Before he could decide if there was even a hint of flirtation in her response, her expression grew serious again and she reached for the door. "Thank you again," she said, her tone now politely dismissive.

"You're welcome." He stepped outside and glanced back at her. "Have a nice…"

The door closed in his face.

"…day," he finished wryly. Shaking his

head, he turned to leave. He had a class to get to that evening. He didn't have time to stand around mooning over a pretty, but decidedly distant, scientist.

"So, you've really had a lousy week," Julia observed, reaching for a tortilla chip to dip into the salsa that sat on the restaurant table in front of her. "First you spent your birthday alone, and then everything in your apartment broke. Not to mention a difficult week at work."

Catherine took a sip of her punch and set the plastic tumbler back down on the table before replying to her friend of almost two years. "It wasn't so bad, really. I received some lovely gifts for my birthday. Thank you again for the gloves, by the way. They're gorgeous."

"You're welcome. I'm just sorry I had to be away on that business trip and couldn't celebrate with you. A girl shouldn't be by herself on her thirtieth birthday."

"Norman and I had a very nice little private party."

"The cat doesn't count."

"Don't tell *him* that," Catherine advised with a smile. "Norman is very sensitive, you know. And as for things breaking in my apartment, that turned out okay, too. The management responded very quickly each time, having the repairs done the very day I reported the problems."

"Wow. That is efficient. I hope you didn't have to deal with gripey old Luther again."

Catherine concentrated on scooping a tortilla chip into white cheese dip, keeping her voice casual when she replied, "Actually, no. There's a new maintenance guy now. His name's Mike."

"Really. Nice guy?"

"Yes, he seems very nice."

A sudden, rather loaded silence from the other side of the table made Catherine look up. "What?"

"How did he look?"

She started to give a vaguely generic answer, but then she sighed and said, "Like he just stepped off a surfboard. Or—since we're a ten-hour drive from the nearest beach—a skateboard, maybe."

"Young guy, huh?"

"I'm not very good at guessing ages, but I'd say twenty-five. Maybe a year or two older."

"And you say he's nice looking?"

"Like someone you would see on the cover of one of those teen magazines my mother would never let me buy," she replied with an exaggerated sigh. "Blond, blue-eyed, athletic build, beautiful smile. Nice teeth. And enough charm to sell sand in a desert."

Julia shuddered. "Sounds like one of those guys who are about as deep as a rain puddle."

Julia had a well-known aversion to handsome, shallow men, having been hurt very badly by one in her younger, more trusting days.

"He seemed quite nice, actually. But—as always happens when I'm in the presence of a good-looking guy—I displayed the wit and personality of petrified wood."

Julia rolled her eyes. "I doubt it was quite that bad."

"Trust me," she said with a groan. "I couldn't even remember poor Norman's name. All I could do was just sit there, staring at the guy. He probably thinks I'm the most boring tenant in the entire complex."

"Oh well, it isn't as if you'd be interested in boffing the maintenance stud, anyway," Julia said with a shrug. "You've got more common sense than that."

"No, of course I wouldn't be interested in anything like that," Catherine agreed with a laugh that sounded a bit hollow to her own ears.

"And he hardly sounds like the kind of man you'd want to date for any other purpose. A young maintenance man? What on earth would you have in common with him?"

Julia, bless her, was pretty much as clueless as Catherine when it came to men. A natural blonde who defied all the stereotypes, she was a fiercely focused and ambitious dynamo in a deceptively fragile-looking package. Unlike Catherine, Julia was frequently the target of passes from prowling males, few of them interested in her mind. Her experiences with the opposite sex had left her decidedly cynical when it came to romance.

Losing interest in the subject of buff young men—and totally oblivious to the man who was openly ogling her from a table nearby—Julia launched into a discussion of a workshop she had attended at the conference in New York. Catherine was quite sure her friend had rarely, if ever, left the conference hotel to enjoy all the wonderfully exciting things to do in the "Big Apple." For Julia, nothing in the city was as interesting and challenging as scholarly discussions of the law.

Hopeless, Catherine thought with a slight shake of her head. Both of them.

Settling in for an evening of spicy Mexican food and stimulating conversation, she pushed the lingering thoughts of Mike Clancy to the back of her mind. She knew full well those thoughts would be there to tease her again later, when she was alone in her apartment.

Friday afternoon Catherine was sitting at her desk behind a mountain of paperwork for an important grant, when she accidentally overheard a couple of graduate students chatting out in the hallway. Maybe they didn't know she was in her office, or maybe they weren't aware of how clearly their voices carried through the partially opened door.

"Got big plans for the weekend?"

"Uh-huh. Scott's taking me to Tunica for a weekend at the casinos. We're leaving tomorrow morning. I can't wait."

"Sounds like fun."

"I know. What are you doing this weekend?"

"Going clubbing tonight with Tommy and Jan and Nick. Tomorrow Tommy and I are driving up to Jonesboro for the football game and staying the night there."

"Cool."

"You and Scott want to go clubbing with us tonight?"

"Maybe. I'll ask him and give you a call."

There was a momentary pause before one of them said, "What do you think *she's* doing this weekend?"

"Dr. Travis? Same thing she does every weekend. Working."

"Think she ever just cuts loose and has fun?"

A laugh of disbelief was followed by a cynical, "I think *fun* might be one of the few words missing from her extensive vocabulary. She's nice and all, but can you imagine her partying?"

"No. The image just won't form in my mind."

The voices faded as the unseen speakers moved down the hallway, leaving an echo of laughter behind them. Only after she was sure they were gone did Catherine get up to quietly close her door.

By the time she arrived at home that evening, her steps were dragging. Though it was after seven, it was still light. The days were getting shorter, though, she mused with a sigh, tucking her bulging briefcase beneath her arm. Soon it would be dark when she came home alone. And cold.

Locking her car door, she glanced across the mostly empty parking lot. Most of the other tenants were already home from work, and quite a few of them had probably already headed out for Friday night fun. Someone climbed out of the driver's side of a small pickup truck, and she recognized Mike, the maintenance man. He seemed to be carrying a stack of books, but he managed to free a hand to give her a quick wave.

She waved back, hoping she looked friendly and casual rather than stiff and self-conscious, and then she turned toward the outside stairs that led up to her second-floor apartment. She smiled when she glanced up and spotted Norman sitting in his favorite spot on the living room windowsill, watching her.

At least someone was glad to welcome her home, she thought, walking a bit faster.

She unlocked her door and pushed it open, thinking that maybe she would throw on some sweats and make an omelet for dinner....

For the first time since she had brought him home six months ago, Norman dashed past her through the open doorway and streaked down the stairs, straight into the parking lot. Terrified that he would run in front of a car, Catherine threw down her bags and raced after him, calling his name. "Norman, stop! Come back here."

Alerted by her shout, Mike got to Norman first, dropping his books to scoop the cat into his arms. Rather than resisting, Norman butted his head happily against Mike's chin, as if in greeting.

Her heart still pounding against her ribs, Catherine skidded to a stop in front of them. "I can't believe he did that. He's never run out before. Thank you so much for catching him."

"No problem." Smiling, Mike transferred her pet into her arms. "Guess you'd better start blocking the door when you open it."

"I guess so." Catherine frowned down at Norman, who was purring as if he were quite pleased with himself. "Bad cat. You could have been hurt."

"So could you, the way you pelted down those stairs," Mike told her. "You're lucky you didn't trip."

She wrinkled her nose. "I didn't even think about it," she confessed. "I was so afraid he would run in front of a car."

As if to emphasize what could have happened, an SUV passed them at that moment, the driver nodding to Mike in recognition. Mike waved back, then turned again to Catherine. "So, how's it going—other than escaping cats? Everything in working order in your apartment?"

"Yes, thank you." She glanced down at the three hardcover books scattered at their feet. "I hope none of your books are damaged. If so, I'll certainly pay for replacements."

"Hey, don't worry about it. They're just textbooks, and I bought them used, anyway." He crouched to gather them, and Catherine couldn't help but notice the titles.

"Biology and American history. You're taking classes?" As soon as the words left her mouth, she cursed her own stupidity. Of course he was taking classes—why else would he be carrying textbooks?

But he merely nodded as he straightened. "I'm taking a couple of classes at UALR." He pronounced it "you-ler," as many locals did.

She wasn't sure what to say, except, "Are they going well?"

He started to nod, then stopped himself with

a grimace. "History's fine. Biology's kicking my butt."

"Really? Anything in particular?"

"We're having a test on glycolysis Monday, and to be honest, it doesn't make a lick of sense to me. I'm going to try to study this weekend, but I have a sinking suspicion it isn't going to help much. I can't make heads or tails of this stuff."

She would never know what impulse made her open her mouth and blurt, "I'll help you."

He looked at her with a curiously lifted eyebrow. "Um—what?"

She told herself that it would make her look even more foolish to take her words back now. And why should she, really? After all, he'd done the favor of helping her rescue Norman. And this was certainly something she was qualified to offer him in return.

"I'll help you study for the test…if you're interested. My undergraduate degree was in biology. So if there's anything I can do to help you prepare—"

"Hey, I'm not too proud to beg for help," he

said with a devastatingly attractive, crooked grin. "If you're sure you have the time, and it isn't too much trouble, I would be grateful for any help you can give me. I really want to pass this test."

She nodded. "It's no trouble at all. When would you like to come by?"

"Are you free tomorrow afternoon?"

"I have some things to do at work in the morning, but I should be home by about two. Shall we make it three o'clock?"

"I'll be there. And, hey, thanks, Dr. Travis. I really appreciate this."

She glanced down at the cat dozing content-edly in her arms, purring like a chain saw. "It's the least I can do. I'll see you tomorrow, then."

Eager now to get away before she said something incredibly dumb, she carried Norman up the stairs to her apartment. When she glanced down from her front door, she noticed that Mike was already gone.

Chapter Two

"Hey, Mike! Heads up."

He turned just in time to snatch the basketball out of the air, spin and sink it into a basket above his head. Nothing but net.

Three male voices groaned loudly. Two others cheered. Mike's three-on-three teammates slapped him on the back and offered upraised hands for high fives.

"And that would be…game!" Bob Sharp performed an embarrassingly dorky dance of victory, his near-shoulder-length red hair flying around his square-jawed face.

"Dude." Mike rolled his eyes. "Chill."

"Seriously."   Black-haired,   green-eyed Brandon Williams, the third member of the winning team, tossed a sweaty towel at Bob. "You're making us look bad."

Still joking around with his teammates and opponents—also all friends—Mike moved to a bench at one side of the park basketball court and rooted in his gym bag for his watch. He groaned when he found it. He had lost track of time during the game and now he had ten minutes to shower, change, grab his books and make it to Catherine Travis's apartment by three o'clock.

He was going to be late.

"Hey, Mike. Wanna go have a beer and watch a game or two?"

"Can't," he replied to Bob's suggestion. "Gotta study."

Typically, Bob brushed off the excuse. "C'mon, man, you can study later. It's not like you'll be grounded if you don't get an A."

He laughed heartily at his own joke. Bob still

couldn't understand why Mike had decided to go back to school almost ten years after dropping out of his first attempt at higher education. Bob was perfectly happy driving a delivery truck and stocking snack machines in local businesses, spending his leisure hours hanging with friends and chasing women.

Until a few months ago, Mike had been pretty much content with that lifestyle himself. Now that he had decided he wanted more, some of his friends seemed determined to try to talk him out of it.

"C'mon, Mike, have a beer with us," Brandon seconded. "It's too nice a day to study."

"Sorry, guys. Can't. I'm supposed to meet someone at three for a study session, and I'm already running late."

"Oh, ho." Bob gave a sudden, knowing grin. "That explains your hurry to hit the books. So who is she?"

"Just someone who offered to help me get ready for a test Monday. And I've really got to go, guys. See you later, okay?"

"You're holding out on us, Clancy," Bob called after him. "We want to meet this chick."

As he jumped into his pickup and threw it into gear, Mike wondered how Dr. Travis would feel about having herself referred to as a "chick." He wouldn't think she'd care for it much.

Dr. Travis. It felt sort of odd to refer to her that way. Made her sound like one of his stuffy professors, rather than the attractive young woman she was.

Glancing at the dashboard clock, he saw that it was almost straight-up three o'clock. He was definitely going to be late.

He had been criticized quite often for his rather fluid concept of time. His friends had pretty much gotten used to never knowing when to expect him. He hoped Dr. Travis wasn't one of those clock-watching types who got upset about that sort of thing.

But when she opened her door for him at twenty minutes after three, she didn't look at all annoyed. In fact, strangely enough, she seemed almost apologetic.

"It occurred to me a few minutes ago that I never gave you my phone number," she said, motioning him inside. "There was no way for you to let me know you'd been held up. I hope you didn't have to rush too hard to get here because of my oversight."

She really was blaming herself because he was late. Interesting. "It's my fault for letting time get away from me," he assured her. "I hope it didn't cause you any inconvenience."

"No. I don't have any other plans for the afternoon." She motioned toward her small, rectangular dining table. "I thought we could spread your books and notes on the table. Can I get you a glass of fresh lemonade before we get started?"

"That sounds great, Dr. Travis. If it's no trouble."

She smiled and shook her head. "I'd like a glass, myself. And please call me Catherine."

He watched surreptitiously as she moved into the kitchen. Wearing an olive-green camp shirt open over a khaki-colored pullover and khaki slacks, she looked even younger than she had the last time he'd seen her. He still couldn't really guess her age, though he would bet she wasn't more than a couple of years on either side of thirty. Very close to his own age.

She must have earned her doctorate at a young age. One of those brainy, ambitious, super-focused types, apparently. But not an intellectual snob. She wasn't giving off any vibes that suggested she considered herself superior to a twenty-eight-year-old maintenance man with only a few hours of college credit behind him.

Remembering a recent, painful encounter with a woman who had made no secret of her disdain for his current status, he winced.

Something touched his leg. He glanced down just as Catherine's cat meowed a greeting. "Well, hello, Norman. I wondered where you were hiding."

Returning to the table with two glasses of lemonade and a plate of brownies, Catherine slid into the chair beside him. "He's been asleep on my bed. He has to have at least ten naps a day or he gets cranky."

Chuckling, Mike scratched Norman's ears, eliciting a loud purr of approval. He stopped scratching to reach for his lemonade. "This looks great. Homemade brownies?"

Catherine shrugged. "Just the box-mix kind. I was having a snack attack earlier."

Judging by her slender frame, she didn't give in to "snack attacks" that often. But since he didn't feel quite right about checking out her figure when she was offering to help him study, he pulled his gaze away from her and snagged a brownie from the platter.

Catherine motioned toward the textbook and notebook he had tossed on the table. "You said you're studying for a test on glycolysis?"

He nodded and turned his thoughts to business. "Yeah. I brought my study sheets and the practice test the professor gave us. I tried to take the practice test yesterday, but I didn't get very far with it."

"Let me look at the test and your notes and I'll see if I can help you understand it better." She gave a self-deprecating little smile that almost took him back to noticing-how-attractive-she-was territory. "Of course, it's been a few years since I've been tested on this stuff, so I might have to refresh myself a bit."

Norman leaped onto Mike's knees and head-butted his chin. Mike patted him absently.

"Just set him down if he's bugging you," Catherine advised. "He takes a hint fairly well—for a short time, anyway."

"He's fine." Mike opened his notebook. "Here's the sample test.…"

"Okay, see if you can answer this one." Catherine said almost an hour later. "Regulation of glycolysis takes place by the a, allosteric inhibition of phosphofructokinase by excess ATP, or b, conversion of dihydroxyacetone phosphate to glyceraldehyde phosphate?"

Mike blinked a couple of times, then frowned in concentration. "That would be…the first one, I think. A."

She smiled at him. "Yes. You're right."

He made a production of wiping his brow,

his self-satisfied smile so endearing that she had to swallow before asking the next question. "Complete this sentence. When yeast cells metabolize glucose anaerobically, the end product is—?"

"Pyruvic acid." He must have seen from her expression that he'd given the wrong answer. He corrected it immediately. "Ethyl alcohol."

She smiled again. "Correct. You're doing very well, Mike. You should have no problem passing this test. Would you like to practice the essay questions? I can busy myself with something else while you work on them and then give my opinion of your answers when you've finished. Of course, you know that essay questions are often graded subjectively, so your professor might judge your responses differently than I would."

"Hey, I'd really appreciate that, if you've got the time. The essay questions really worry me. It's been almost ten years since I've had to write essays, and to be honest, I wasn't very good at it back then."

"No problem. I have a couple of journal articles I need to read. I can do that while you write. I'll let you know when your allotted time is up."

He nodded and drained the last of his second glass of lemonade, then bent industriously over his notebook.

Catherine studied him for a moment, then stood and moved to the sofa. She picked up one of the journals sitting on the coffee table. Norman padded across the floor to jump into her lap, kneading her thigh while she turned to the article she had marked earlier.

Rubbing the spot between his shoulder blades that always made him arch in bliss, she tried to keep her eyes on the page. It wasn't easy. Mike just looked so darned good sitting at her table, his blond-streaked hair all tousled, a frown of concentration on his pretty face. She sighed.

He glanced around. "Everything okay?"

"Fine," she assured him a bit too heartily. "Norman's just being a little too enthusiastic with the claws."

He smiled, then looked back down at his

notebook. She turned her own attention firmly to the page in front of her.

She knew she would never be able to concentrate on the complex article with Mike sitting so close by, so she entertained herself by imagining how her cousin Lori, the biggest flirt she knew, would behave with a handsome man in her apartment. Lori would certainly not be sitting on the far side of the room pretending to read a scientific journal, that was for certain!

Because she didn't know how to be any other way, Catherine was completely honest with her appraisal of Mike's essay answers. She figured she would be wasting both their time if she didn't make a genuine effort to help him. She tempered her criticism with praise for the things he had done well, but she made no effort to pander to his ego when she pointed out the areas that would very likely lose him points with his professor.

"This is worded too vaguely," she said, underlining one weak paragraph. "And here you've gotten off topic, which would get points marked off by most professors, since they don't like wasting grading time. And this statement is simply incorrect. In eukaryotes, the enzymes involved in the Krebs cycle and electron transport are located in the mitochondria, not the cell membranes as you've written here. This is a very basic biology class, but that's something you should be expected to know already."

Mike winced. Something about his expression made her suspect that he wasn't accustomed to being corrected so bluntly, and she wondered for a moment if she should have made an effort to be more tactful. But then she reminded herself that he surely wanted her to be honest, or he wouldn't have wasted a beautiful Saturday afternoon studying in her apartment. He certainly hadn't come just to spend time with her and Norman.

"Thanks," he said without much enthusiasm. "I'll work on those things."

"I'm sure you'll do very well on the test," she said, in case he was becoming discouraged.

"I hope you're right. It's been harder going back to school than I expected," he admitted.

"To be honest, I flunked out the first time I tried college almost ten years ago, but I told myself it was because I partied too much and studied too little while I was there. I thought maybe if I actually put a little effort into it this time, I'd be more successful with it."

"I'm sure you will. It must be difficult learning how to study again after such a long absence."

"Again?" he repeated with a short laugh. "I *never* learned how to study. Didn't have to in school. My mother and sisters gave me so much 'help' with my homework that I managed to graduate with a minimally adequate grade point average. I got a baseball scholarship to college, but I lost that when the grades fell. It wasn't as if I was ever going to make it to the pros, anyway. I was a decent player, but not exactly star quality."

Catherine wasn't sure what to say in response to his candidness. "What made you decide to go back now?" she asked, then wondered if that had been too personal a question.

His shrug was more sheepish than offended.

"I attended my ten-year high school reunion this summer," he muttered, as if that were explanation enough.

Apparently he had compared himself to some of his classmates and hadn't been pleased with what he had seen. She gave him a wry smile. "Perhaps you should have done what I did. I skipped my ten-year reunion altogether."

"Oh? When was that?" he asked with a casualness that was probably intended to disguise the fact that he was basically asking her age.

"Two years ago. I just turned thirty last Saturday."

"Then I'll wish you a belated happy birthday."

"Thank you."

He leaned back in his chair, slinging one arm over the back. "So why didn't you go to your reunion? I would think you'd be proud to let everyone know you'd turned out so well."

Uncomfortable with the new direction the conversation had taken, and suspecting Mike had deliberately directed it away from himself, she shrugged a little before saying, "I don't have that many fond memories of high school. I wasn't eager to relive my time there."

She suppressed a wince as she finished speaking. Had she sounded bitter? No one enjoyed spending time with a complainer. "I'm sure I would have had a good time if I'd gone," she amended quickly, "but I was at a science convention in London that weekend, anyway."

"Yeah, well, I thought I'd have a great time at my reunion," Mike murmured, looking down at the pencil he was twisting slowly in his left hand. "I mean, I had a fantastic time in high school. Played sports, had a lot of friends. Parties every weekend, hanging out by the lake all summer."

She could almost picture the boy he had been. The jock. One of the popular crowd. Strutting through the halls of his high school with the kind of confidence that most adolescents could only watch and secretly envy. She didn't want to believe that he had been one of the cruel kids. The ones who mocked and belittled anyone who didn't fit into their narrow definition of what was acceptable. What was cool.

No, Mike had probably been carelessly nice to everyone. Perhaps a bit oblivious to the ones on the outskirts of the in-crowd. He wouldn't have been the type to be deliberately cruel to them; he simply hadn't noticed them very often, she thought with a sigh.

"Catherine?"

"Oh, sorry," she said, realizing she'd been quiet for too long. "Flashback to my own school years, I guess. So, your reunion wasn't as much fun as you expected?"

He shrugged. "Not quite. Most of my classmates have moved on, left those years behind. The ones who haven't—who sat around all day drinking and replaying old memories and talking about how high school was the high point of their lives—well, they just seemed sort of pathetic, you know?"

He must have experienced quite an epiphany at that reunion. She was a little surprised that he was being so frank about it now, to her, a virtual stranger.

Perhaps he had also revealed more than he had

intended. With a quick, rather irritated shake of his head, he began to gather his books and papers. "So you think I'll ace this test now, huh?"

"I'm not sure you'll ace it, exactly, but I'm sure you'll do very—oh. You were teasing." And she had responded with a careful earnestness that he must have found equally naive and clueless. She had been accused on more than one occasion of being a bit challenged when it came to a sense of humor.

To give him credit, there was no mockery in his smile. "Yeah, I was teasing. Trust me, I'd be happy with a C."

"It wouldn't hurt to *try* to ace it," she responded, thinking he was selling himself too short. "I've always been told that confidence is the greatest part of success."

Tucking his books beneath one arm, he smiled. "There are plenty of people who would tell you that I've never lacked for confidence."

Somehow she suspected that no matter how many people agreed with him on that point, it wasn't exactly true—not when it came to certain aspects of his life. But she would bet he was quite adept at camouflaging any inse- curities he might have.

It was odd to think of a man like this suffer- ing self-doubts. And rather ironic that their doubts were in such dramatically opposite areas. He was entirely comfortable in social situations; she had never worried about academic pursuits.

He was obviously ready to leave. She moved toward the door. "Good luck with your test, Mike."

"Thanks. It was really nice of you to help me study."

"You're quite welcome," she said, hating the primness she heard in her own voice.

He bent to scratch her cat's ears. "See you around, Norman."

With a smile that included both her and the cat—and didn't seem to particularly favor either of them, she thought regretfully—he let himself out.

Norman remained in his position for several long moments, staring at the closed door with wide, unblinking eyes. It was only when she realized that she was doing much the same thing that Catherine prodded herself into motion. "Give it up, Norman. He's not coming back."

The cat didn't move. Shaking her head in rueful amusement, Catherine moved to the kitchen to put away the glasses she and Mike had used. Before setting Mike's glass in the dishwasher, she indulged herself in one moment of fantasy by touching a fingertip to the rim. His lips might have touched just there, she mused. It was only her imagination, of course, that made the glass feel a bit warmer in that spot.

He did have a nicely shaped mouth. His upper lip was sensually curved, and his lower lip was just full enough to be nibble-able. When he smiled, as he did so often and so easily, his teeth flashed white and even, and there was just a hint of a dimple at the right corner of his mouth. When he'd tipped his head back to drink his lemonade, his tanned throat had worked with his swallows, calling her attention to the vee of the nicely fitted knit shirt he'd worn with comfortably loose jeans.

Sighing lightly, she set the glass on the dishwasher rack and shut the door. It was silly for her to be standing here mooning over him like an infatuated schoolgirl. And yet…it felt sort of good. It was nice to know her libido was still in working order, despite the amount of time that had passed since she'd last made use of it.

It had been a pleasant couple of hours. She hadn't made a fool of herself, and she had managed to uphold her end of the conversation even when they hadn't been talking about science. She'd even managed to crack a couple of jokes and make him smile a couple of times—not that Mike's smiles were exactly rare.

Maybe if she'd had a bit more practice at that sort of interaction with attractive men, she wouldn't have celebrated her birthday with her cat, she thought wistfully.

Chapter Three

Mike couldn't remember ever feeling so confident leaving a classroom after a test. It was almost as if Catherine had known exactly what his professor was going to ask and had drilled him specifically on those points. He had found himself thinking of her during the exam, hearing her voice explaining the concepts to him as he'd read the questions.

He wasn't quite cocky enough to believe he'd aced the thing, but he was quite certain he had passed. He wouldn't be at all surprised to have earned better than an average grade. It was a good feeling. And he had Catherine to thank for it.

He had to stop by the supermarket on his way home. He was out of sodas and frozen waffles, his usual breakfast staples. Impulse made him wander into the florist section while he was there.

Half an hour later he stood outside Catherine's door, having a few second thoughts about being there at all. He didn't want her to start thinking of him as a nuisance. Maybe he should just forget about this and…

Her door opened before he had a chance to decide whether to ring the bell. Catherine came very close to barreling straight into him before she stopped herself with a gasp of surprise.

"Oh. Mike," she said, flustered. "I didn't know you were here."

"You're on your way out," he commented unnecessarily, suddenly awkward. "I won't keep you. I just wanted to give you these. You know, as a thank-you for helping me with my studying."

She looked a bit startled when he handed her the inexpensive bouquet of mixed blooms. Was it because she wasn't accustomed to receiving flowers from her handyman? Was she wondering uncomfortably if there was more to the gesture than simple gratitude?

"It's no big deal," he said quickly when she tried to stammer a thank-you. "I was at the supermarket, feeling pretty good about my test, and I saw the flowers and thought I should do something to repay you for your help. Since you wouldn't take any real pay, I mean."

She had, in fact, quite firmly rebuffed his offer to pay her for her tutoring services.

Her smile seemed to dim just a bit, but her tone was sincere when she said, "I'm glad to hear the test went well. When will you know your grade?"

"The professor is going to post them on his Web site tomorrow. I really think I did well, Catherine. I wouldn't be surprised if I got a B. High C at the lowest."

She smiled up at him. "That's very good news."

She really did have pretty eyes. Such a rich, dark brown that he could see his own reflection in them. He lowered his gaze to her mouth. And found himself captured for a moment by the soft curve of her upper lip.

He cleared his throat, using the sound to bring his own wandering thoughts back on track. "I won't keep you any longer," he said. "I hope I didn't cause you to be late."

Wrinkling her nose a little, she shook her head. "I'm just headed for the lab. I've got an experiment going, and I'll probably be there until after midnight."

He was a bit surprised. "Don't you have grad students to handle that sort of thing?"

She smiled again. "I'm only an associate professor, just two years out of my postdoctoral position. I have a grad student assigned to my lab, but she has her own research to do. We have a lab tech, but he can't handle what I need to do tonight. So…it's up to me."

"How many hours a week do you work?"

She shrugged. "Anywhere from forty to eighty hours a week. Research isn't a nine-to-five, five-day-a-week job. But it also gives me some flexibility with my work hours when I have appointments or errands to run or just need some time away from the lab."

A hard worker, this one, he thought. Smart, focused, self-sufficient. He admired the heck out of her. And if he were perfectly honest with himself, he would admit that he was just a little intimidated by her. And *that* was a new experience for him.

"Well…" He took a step backward. "Don't work too hard."

"Thank you again for the flowers."

He noticed that she had her nose buried in the bouquet when she turned away and closed the door. She seemed to really like the flowers. He was glad now that he had given in to his impulse to buy them.

"And I've put in almost seventy hours on that one case this week," Julia announced.

Stabbing her fork into a grilled scallop, Catherine replied with the expected murmur of amazement. Yet she knew her friend wasn't actually complaining. There was nothing Julia enjoyed more than a challenging legal case.

A burst of laughter from somewhere behind her interrupted their quiet conversation. It wasn't the first time it had happened. "That group behind me is certainly enjoying the evening," she commented without looking around.

"Looks like a birthday party or something," Julia said, glancing past Catherine's shoulder. "Big group."

"Must be that redhead's birthday," Karen Kupperman remarked from the other side of the table. "Everyone seems to be looking at her."

"They'd probably be doing that even if it wasn't her birthday," Julia replied matter-of-factly. "She's gorgeous."

"She is, isn't she?" chubby, pleasantly plain, thirty-five-year-old Karen agreed without envy. "Love that blouse she's wearing. I wonder if it comes in my size."

Because her back was turned to the people in question, Catherine had nothing to add to the conversation. She took a bite of fish, savoring the light seasoning.

"Speaking of birthdays," Karen went on as if it were a perfectly logical segue, "I'm sorry again I wasn't here to help you celebrate yours, Catherine."

"You had an excellent excuse." Karen had just returned from her two-week trip to Europe, the long-overdue vacation following a science research conference. Catherine had already thanked Karen for the birthday gift and had seen the photos from the European trip.

Karen was obviously eager to talk more about her vacation. Catherine resigned herself to hearing several mildly amusing anecdotes again. She didn't really mind, since she was pleased that Karen had enjoyed the trip so much. Still, it was yet another reminder that while Catherine had celebrated alone with her cat, other people had been having much more interesting adventures.

As if to underline that thought, another burst of laughter came from behind them.

Julia glanced that way again, then said to

Karen, "Has Catherine told you about the maintenance guy she's been seeing?"

Effectively distracted from her vacation reminiscences—which had probably been Julia's intention—Karen turned to Catherine with a look that combined equal parts disbelief and intrigue. "No, this is the first I've heard of a maintenance guy. What is she talking about, Catherine?"

"She is being ridiculous," Catherine replied with a chiding look at Julia. "I haven't been 'seeing' anyone."

"Mmm." Julia's expression betrayed her skepticism. "And the flowers he gave you yesterday?"

"Simply a thank-you for helping him study for his test," Catherine retorted. She hoped her tart tone hid the ripple of pleasure that went through her at the mention of that bouquet. She never should have mentioned the flowers to Julia, of course, but it had been such a nice and completely unexpected gesture that she hadn't been able to resist sharing it with her friend when Julia had called earlier to set the time for this dinner.

Karen lifted both eyebrows. "None of my students give me flowers for extra tutoring."

"He isn't a student," Julia corrected. "He's the maintenance man at her apartment complex. And, though I've never seen him, I've gotten the impression that he is *very* nice looking."

"I barely know him," Catherine said to Karen, who was still eyeing her in question. "He came to fix something in my apartment, and he happened to mention that he was having trouble studying for a college biology test. I offered to help him, and he spent a couple of hours at my apartment Saturday. He brought me a small bouquet yesterday as a way of thanking me because he believed he'd done well on the exam. End of story."

Karen sighed. "Throw me a crumb here. Is he at least good-looking, as Julia suggested?"

Catherine hesitated, then gave Julia another look before conceding, "Well, yes. He's very nice looking. Not that it matters, of course."

Groaning, Karen waved a finger at her. "Have I taught you nothing? Of *course* it matters."

Because Wayne Kupperman bore a distinct resemblance to the doughboy character on television commercials, Catherine knew Karen was only teasing about looks being important. She smiled obligingly.

"Still, a college student?" Karen shook her head. "I don't think you're quite reduced to cradle robbing."

"It's not like that. He's gone back to school after several years away. He's twenty-eight. Still a little younger than I am, but…" Realizing what she was saying, Catherine stopped with a sigh. "That doesn't matter, either. There is absolutely nothing going on, Karen."

"Let me get this straight. He's close to your age, good-looking, nice enough to bring you flowers—and you aren't interested in him?"

Because she couldn't honestly deny any interest in him, Catherine spoke a bit more tartly than she intended when she said, "Mike and I obviously have absolutely nothing in common. Even if I *were* interested, nothing's going to happen."

"So maybe you aren't soul mates. You could still enjoy yourself with a harmless flirtation, couldn't you?"

Julia, who had appeared to be concentrating on her meal, glanced up then. "Catherine doesn't know how to flirt. She commented about that just the other night."

"You're one to talk," Karen, who had known Julia since college and had been the one to introduce her to Catherine a couple of years earlier, remarked pointedly. "You never even notice when anyone flirts with you."

"I know," Julia answered matter-of-factly. "Someone always has to tell me later that I was being hit on."

"Hopeless," Karen proclaimed. "The two of you. It isn't exactly rocket science, girls."

"Rocket science would be less intimidating to me." Catherine reached for her water glass. "And, anyway, who are you to give advice on flirting or dating? You've hardly ever dated anyone but Wayne. You told me you were college sweethearts from your freshman year and his junior year, for heaven's sake. You got married while you were both still in graduate school."

Karen had to concede that point. "If Wayne and I should split up, I wouldn't have a clue how to get back into the dating scene. I guess I'd better just keep him."

As if that were even a question. With the exception of her own parents, Catherine had never met any couple more suited than Karen and Wayne.

"They really should offer classes in that sort of thing," Karen went on thoughtfully. She nodded toward the boisterous group in the back corner of the big dining room. "The birthday redhead there could probably be the professor."

Though she tried to be subtle about it, Catherine couldn't resist craning her neck around to get a glimpse of the woman both Julia and Karen had pointed out. She spotted the redhead immediately, and she could see why her friends had noticed her.

The woman really was lovely. Her hair was a rich strawberry blond, cascading in a silky curtain to her shoulders, which were all but bared by the royal-blue, halter-neck dress she wore. Her face was a perfect oval of creamy porcelain, warmed by big, laughing green eyes and a vivid smile.

Just looking at her made Catherine feel dowdy and plain in her tailored white blouse and gray slacks, her own brown hair styled in its usual neat bob. While Julia might be technically as pretty as the redhead, her clothes were much more sedate, her expression more keep-your-distance than come-hither. And Karen... As fond as she was of her, Catherine had to admit that few men would look twice at matronly Karen if that redhead was in the same room. At herself, either, for that matter.

"She really is beautiful." Again, there wasn't a trace of envy in Karen's voice. "And would you look at that guy with her. Is he a perfect specimen or what?"

"Which guy?" Julia asked without much interest. "There are four of them."

Not wanting to be caught staring, Catherine had turned back around after glancing at the redhead. She hadn't really noticed any of the men in the birthday party.

"The blond one," Karen said, gazing openly in that direction. "Green shirt. Looks like he should be on the cover of a magazine."

"Oh. Him." Julia's voice chilled several degrees. "He looks like a jerk. One of those guys who thinks he's such hot stuff that he can get away with anything."

Catherine shook her head in exasperation with her friend's attitude. Julia had no patience for shallow, frivolous people— although she had good reason. She had encountered too many men who had pretended to be interested in her brains and competence, when what they had really wanted was a beautiful blonde to dangle from their arms. A woman who excelled in a field once dominated by men, Julia hated to be patronized, trivialized or underestimated. And she said she was treated that way most often by slick, handsome men.

"Let's just forget about that other group,"

Catherine suggested. "The three of us don't get that many opportunities to have a leisurely dinner together. We should make the most of it."

The conversation had just drifted back to Karen's vacation when the group behind them began to sing the happy birthday song. Julia looked up from her dessert with a slight frown. "They certainly are loud."

"They're just having fun," Karen said, glancing that way with an indulgent smile.

Catherine turned again to look in that direction, as were most of the other diners in the restaurant. They had been right about it being the redhead's birthday. She was glowing as her friends sang to her.

Remembering Karen and Julia's earlier conversation, Catherine scanned the group idly for the man who had caused Karen to sigh and Julia to scowl. A blond man, they had said. Sitting close to the...

Her gaze froze, and she felt her smile slide right off her face.

She wasn't sure what made him look suddenly

her way. Simply coincidence, perhaps. But suddenly he spotted her, and recognition dawned instantly on his face. His smile widened, and he gave her a little wave. Catherine waved a bit stiffly in return, then turned quickly back to her dinner companions.

"Catherine, do you know that guy?" Karen asked curiously. "He's the one Julia and I were talking about."

"Yes, I know him."

"Really? Someone from work? I don't recognize him."

"No. Someone from my apartment complex."

Karen's eyes widened comically. "Oh, surely not."

"Surely not what?" Julia asked, as clueless as ever.

"That's the one who brought you flowers?" Karen demanded.

Catherine nodded. "How did you guess?"

"Let's face it. How many men do you know who fit that description?"

"You have a point there."

"That's the maintenance guy?" Julia asked, catching up. She looked toward Mike's table again and shook her head. "I see what you mean, now, about nothing happening between you. He would be totally wrong for you."

Even though Julia was only repeating what Catherine, herself, had been saying, Catherine was aware of a sudden, sinking feeling inside her. "It's hardly necessary for you to tell me that."

"Oh, I don't know." Karen frowned at Julia. "I think it might be good for Catherine to get out of her rut. She wouldn't have to marry the guy or anything, but why shouldn't she have fun?"

"Waste of time," Julia said dismissively. "Catherine's a woman with a demanding career. Why would she want to complicate her life even more when she knows it won't lead anywhere? Guy like that, first time she has to blow him off for job demands, he'll sulk. Next time it happens, as we all know it will, he'll take off in search of someone who has nothing better to do than to cater to his ego."

"You aren't being fair, Julia. You don't even know this man."

"Trust me. I know dozens of this man."

"You're so cynical. Even for a lawyer."

"Yeah, well, it's easy for you to be all starry-eyed. You married the only Mr. Perfect and left the rest of us with the jerks and the losers."

"Wayne isn't perfect." But then Karen smiled, her plain face suddenly almost pretty. "But I'll admit that he's darned close."

"Just because this Mike guy is pretty and gave her flowers doesn't mean Catherine should get tangled up with him."

Catherine cleared her throat rather forcefully. "I *am* still here, you know. I can hear every word of this totally inane conversation."

Karen giggled. "We haven't forgotten about you."

"Then could we change the subject now, please?" Though she knew it was foolish, she had the unsettling feeling that Mike would somehow know they were talking about him.

Karen looked a bit reluctant, but Julia was

more than happy to veer the conversation into a new direction. Very aware of Mike sitting on the other side of the room, but trying to pretend she had forgotten all about him, Catherine focused intently on her friends as they finished their meals.

Catherine spotted Mike across the apartment compound as she climbed out of her car late the next afternoon. A toolbox in his hands, he was chatting with an older man she knew to be a longtime resident. Other tenants were moving around the parking lot, either walking to or away from their vehicles. She noted that several of them called out greetings to Mike, to which he responded with cordial waves.

He had certainly made himself known during his brief time on this job. She had lived here almost two years and knew the names of maybe three of her neighbors.

Finishing his conversation, he turned her way, saw her and lifted his hand in a wave. She paused in the shade of the oak tree next to her apartment building when he indicated that he wanted to speak with her.

"How's it going?" he asked as he approached her.

"Very well, thank you. And you?"

"Not bad. I just wanted to tell you I got a B on my biology exam. A high B, just two points away from an A. The professor graded off on one of my essay questions," he added with a charmingly sheepish smile. "Said I was 'too vague.'"

She returned the smile, feeling safe to tease him a bit since he seemed to have accepted the comments good-naturedly. "Imagine that."

He chuckled. "You did try to warn me."

"Still, a high B is an excellent grade. Congratulations."

"Thanks." He looked genuinely proud of himself.

"When's your next exam?"

"Friday."

"Do you feel good about it?"

He hesitated just a moment before smiling a bit too brightly. "Oh, yeah. Piece of cake."

Tilting her head, she studied him with a frown. "What will it cover?"

"Classification of organisms. You know, prokaryotes and eukaryotes. Real basic stuff that everyone should know by college."

And yet he didn't sound at all confident that he did know the material that well. "I'd be happy to quiz you, if you like," she offered diffidently. "Not that I'm implying you're not ready, of course, but—"

"You're sure? Because I wouldn't want to be a nuisance to you. I really don't expect you to help me study for every test."

"I don't mind," she assured him. "This is a fairly slow week for me—which is a rarity, actually. I can spare a couple of hours to talk about plantae and such."

"Eukaryotes, right?"

She smiled again. "Right. When's a good time for you?"

"I have a class this evening. But I'm free tomorrow evening, if that's good for you."

"Yes, fine. I should be home by six."

"Do you like pizza?"

The non sequitur made her blink, but she nodded. "Yes."

"Then I'll bring dinner." He dug into his shirt pocket, pulled out a card and a pen, and scribbled on the back. "Here's my cell number, in case something comes up. Don't feel obligated for this if there's something else you need to do."

Even as she gave him her numbers in exchange, she couldn't imagine anything cropping up that would be more tempting than having pizza and studying with Mike Clancy.

Chapter Four

"Hey, Catherine. You'll be here this evening, won't you? Would you mind pulling a couple of plates for me?"

Catherine looked up from her microscope in response to the question the next afternoon. It was from one of the young women she had overheard talking about her last week, commenting about how Catherine never did anything but work, as if she had no life outside the lab.

It gave her great satisfaction to be able to say, "I'm sorry, Brandy, I won't be here this evening. I have a date."

"A date?"

Catherine wasn't flattered by the surprise in the younger woman's expression. She nodded coolly, feeling little compunction now about misrepresenting her plans for the evening. "You'll have to ask someone else."

"Okay…well…have fun."

"Thank you. I intend to."

It wasn't like her to take such pleasure from deliberately misleading someone. But her lips curved into a rather grim smile of satisfaction as she bent back down to her work. It felt good to make it clear that she didn't actually live here in the lab, with no outside interests of her own.

She really was going to have to start getting out more to make that assertion entirely true.

Catherine usually dressed quite casually— pretty much a necessity for most lab work. Her wardrobe consisted primarily of khakis and camp shirts in muted solids, often worn open over beige or white sleeveless tops. When the weather turned cooler, she swapped the camp shirts for thin sweaters with sleeves that could be pushed up and out of her way.

Occasionally she paired her khakis with more-professional blouses and blazers. When she had to dress up, she wore black slacks with the blazers. She rarely wore jeans or shorts and owned only a few skirts, since bare legs were not usually a good idea in a science lab.

Because her wardrobe was so simple and her choices rather limited, she didn't spend much time deciding what to wear. She simply reached for a pair of slacks and any of the dozen or so shirts that matched them. She kept her hair in an easy-to-style bob, wore only light touches of makeup and eschewed all jewelry except her functional watch and a couple of pairs of simply styled earrings. She could be ready to leave her apartment in under half an hour.

All of which made it completely out of character for her to dither about her clothing for almost twenty minutes before Mike arrived Thursday evening. She had gotten home from work an hour earlier than she'd expected, giving her plenty of time to freshen up and change before Mike arrived, but for some reason she couldn't decide what to wear. How silly, considering they wouldn't be doing anything but studying, and that he wouldn't notice her clothes, anyway.

She reached for fresh khakis and camp shirt, then paused again. On an impulse, she turned to a shelf on which she kept the two pairs of jeans that she owned. She donned a pair with a snug-fitting yellow T-shirt, then slid her bare feet into a pair of brown leather clogs.

Eyeing her reflection in the full-length mirror attached to the back of her closet door, she wondered if she had made the right choice. She looked more casual than usual. Too casual? Did it appear as though she were trying too hard to look younger?

"What do you think, Normie?"

The cat, who had been playing with a jingling toy ball near her feet, looked up and meowed rather impatiently, as if to tell her to stop being silly. Deciding that he was right, she turned off the closet light and left the bedroom.

Mike was late again, but only by fifteen minutes. The large pizza box in his hand looked as though it was still steaming, which probably explained his tardiness, she decided. Maybe he'd had to wait in line to pick it up. They should have just called for delivery.

A backpack was slung over one shoulder of the Hawaiian print shirt he wore over a T-shirt and faded jeans, reminding her of the "surfer dude" nickname she had given him the first time she'd seen him. He greeted her with a broad, beaming smile that elicited quivers of reaction deep inside her. "Hi."

"Hi." She moved to one side. "Come in."

She closed the door behind him as he bent to scratch Norman's ears. She wondered if anyone had seen him entering her apartment with the pizza, and if any tongues would wag as a result. She wasn't accustomed to imagining herself at the center of apartment complex chatter, since her life wasn't exactly fodder for juicy gossip.

"The pizza smells really good," she said, making a stab at polite chitchat.

"We should probably eat it while it's still hot, and then study afterward, don't you think?"

"That sounds good. What would you like to drink?" she asked, waving him toward the table.

"Do you have a cola?"

"Only diet, I'm afraid."

"That'll work. It wouldn't hurt me to cut a few calories."

She almost suspected him of saying that just to get her to look at his athletically built body. Even if that hadn't been his intention, it was exactly what she did. Swallowing a comment about how he certainly didn't have to worry about his weight—or anything else about his appearance, for that matter—she moved into the kitchen to fetch plates, napkins and two canned diet sodas.

Catherine had been a bit concerned that conversation might be awkward between herself and Mike while they ate, but Mike took care of that. He had a talent for making small talk that she could only envy. Somehow she found herself relaxing and responding almost as easily as she might have chatted with Karen and Julia.

"Tell me a little about yourself," he urged as he reached for a second slice of pizza. "Where did you grow up? Do you have any brothers or sisters? Did you always want to be a scientist?"

She hesitated a moment to organize her thoughts before answering. "I was born in College Station, Texas, but we moved several times during the next dozen years. My parents are college professors, and they taught in Texas and Virginia and Georgia before settling in Florida when I was twelve. They both taught at Florida State University until Dad retired two years ago, and Mom retired last year. They're spending six months in Beijing now on a cooperative teaching program with the university there. They've been there just over a month."

"How exciting for them."

"Yes, they were thrilled to have this opportunity."

"No siblings?"

"No. My parents had given up on having

children by the time I came along." She re-membered that he was the youngest of five siblings. She couldn't imagine being a part of such a large family. Her own childhood had been quiet and orderly. She had never even had a pet before Norman.

"Was it lonely for you?"

"No, not really. I was very close to my parents and they always saw to it that I had playmates. They enrolled me in very good preschool programs and then excellent private schools as I grew older. Needless to say, they were heavily focused on academic enrichment. I spent every summer in educational camps, studying every-thing from math to science to foreign languages."

"And you liked that?" he asked a bit dubiously.

"I loved it," she admitted with a smile. "I always looked forward to my summer programs. I made friends as well as learned a wide variety of subjects."

"I spent my summers playing ball and working construction jobs for spending money. When I wasn't at the ballpark or on a job site,

I'd be at the pool with my buddies, checking out the girls in bikinis."

Illustrating once again how very different they were, even from childhood.

"When did you decide you wanted to be a scientist?" he asked.

"I don't remember, exactly. My parents always encouraged me to pursue academia." That, of course, was an understatement, since her parents had pretty much mapped out her future from her birth. Fortunately, she had been perfectly willing to go along with their plans, which had suited her temperament well enough. "I suppose I started focusing on the biological sciences as a teenager, when I began to show a particular aptitude for the subject."

"So you never looked at anything else?"

"I briefly considered pursuing an M.D., but I decided against that because I'm too much of a control freak," she admitted. "If I couldn't make the patients do what I suggested, it would make me crazy."

"And you have more control in research?"

She had to laugh at that. "No. Research is usually two steps forward, one step back. Or as often as not, one step forward and three steps back. There are a zillion little variables that can affect any experiment, many of which the researcher has little to no control over."

His gaze seemed to focus for a long moment on her smiling mouth. "That doesn't bother you?"

What bothered her was the look in his eyes just then, an expression she couldn't begin to interpret. She cleared her throat silently and said, "I get frustrated sometimes, but I enjoy my work for the most part."

"Lots of pressure to get results and get published, I would imagine."

"Oh, sure. Add to that the steady dwindling of grant monies for scientific research, and it's a fairly high-stress job. But I can deal with that."

His gaze rose to her eyes again. "Something tells me you can handle just about anything."

No, she thought with a quick ripple of anxiety. There were some things she didn't know how to handle at all.

"So tell me more about your upcoming test," she said a bit too hastily. "Do you feel pretty confident about it?"

A third slice of pizza halfway to his mouth, Mike looked a bit surprised by her abrupt change of subject. "Um—yeah, pretty good. There are a couple of things I'm hoping you can explain a little better for me, but I think I have a good chance at doing well."

Chagrined at her awkwardness, she stuffed a bite of pizza into her mouth and reached grimly for her glass. She had certainly brought that conversation to an abrupt halt.

Maybe she had better just stick to tutoring.

Mike gathered his books and papers and stuffed them into his backpack an hour and a half later. "Once again, you've been really helpful, Catherine. I think I'm ready for the test now."

Catherine stood just a few feet away, watching him prepare to leave. Norman lay bonelessly in her arms, purring so loudly Mike could hear him from where he stood. "You've very welcome. Let me know how it goes, okay? I'll be curious."

"Yes, I will." He was rather pleased by her request, since it indicated a willingness on her part for their budding friendship to continue. He'd thought earlier that perhaps he had blown it by asking too many questions about her. It rather surprised him how important it was for him to keep the lines of communication open between them.

It wasn't because she was helping him study. He liked her. He admired her sharp mind and her generosity. Her cat. And, he had to admit, her chocolatey eyes, sensual mouth and willowy figure.

He hesitated at the door, a bit reluctant to leave. "I forgot to ask, how did you like that new restaurant the other night? I saw you there with your friends."

"I thought it was quite good. My friends and I try to get together for dinner at least once a month, and we're always pleased to find someplace new to eat. I noticed that your group seemed to be having a good time."

He chuckled. "Those were my sister's friends, actually. It was her birthday, so she chose who to invite. But I had a good time with them."

"That beautiful redhead is your sister?" Catherine asked in surprise.

Smiling, he nodded. "That's Laurie. My sister Charlie was also at the table. You might not have seen her because she had her back to you, but she's another redhead."

"Do all your sisters have red hair?"

"Three of the four inherited Dad's red hair. The other sister, the oldest, Gretchen, has the same blond hair that our mother and I have."

"Are they all as pretty as Laurie?"

"Well, I think so—but I'm not exactly objective."

"A very handsome family, apparently."

He couldn't help wondering if she included him in that description. Vain of him, of course, but he would like to think she found him as attractive as she was to him. "I guess I'd better go. Thanks again, Catherine. I wish there was some way that I could repay you."

"You've brought flowers and pizza. That's really plenty."

He couldn't understand what it was about her that made him uncharacteristically tongue-tied. With any other attractive, intriguing woman, he'd have already made his move. Flirted a little, tested her reaction to see if she might be receptive to going out with him. After that... well, he usually just allowed nature to take its course.

Catherine Travis made him feel as awkward and uncertain as a schoolboy who'd never even had his first date. And because he wasn't sure he liked that feeling, he made a swift departure at that point, before he made a complete fool of himself.

Catherine was very busy at work during the next week. She spent long hours in the lab and at her desk, arriving home late and tired, then leaving very early again the next morning. She neither saw nor heard from Mike during that week, nor did she expect to. As reluctant as she was to admit it, she wasn't sure she would ever see him again, except in passing, perhaps, around the complex.

It wasn't as if anything had changed in her life, she told herself as she sat wearily on her couch late Friday evening, trying to get up the energy to get ready for bed. Mike had popped in a few times and had now moved on. He had friends of his own, a big family, work and school. And she was certainly busy with her own job and...

Well, she couldn't say much about her social life, she conceded, looking down at the snoozing cat in her lap. But she did have friends of her own.

Exhausted from the demanding week, she slept later than usual Saturday morning. The telephone rang at 8:00 a.m., causing her to wake with a start and snatch the receiver from its cradle.

"Hello?" The word came out in a croak, making it impossible for her to deny that she had been sleeping.

"You aren't up yet?" Sounding as crisp and alert as ever, Julia was obviously surprised.

"Long week in the lab," Catherine explained after clearing her throat. "I guess I crashed."

"I'm sorry I woke you. Would you like me to call back later?"

"No, it's okay. I'd have been up soon, anyway." Catherine pushed herself upright, dislodging Norman from her pillow.

"I called to ask you a favor. You know that business trip I have to make to Chicago next week? I really need to do some shopping first. My wardrobe is getting pretty pathetic, and you know how I hate to shop."

"Yes, I know." It wasn't Catherine's favorite activity, either.

"So will you go with me? I'd have asked Karen, since she's the shopper of our little group, but she had plans for today."

"Of course, though I'm not sure how much help I'll be. You know I'm pretty clueless when it comes to fashion."

"You'll be my moral support. And you can keep me from strangling perky salespeople."

Catherine chuckled. "Well, I can try."

"So when can you go?"

"I have to run by the lab to check on an experiment, but I can meet you somewhere after lunch. Say, one o'clock?"

"Great." They agreed on a place to meet and then Julia hung up with her usual lack of ceremony.

Catherine yawned, stretched and climbed out of bed. If she was going to get to the lab and meet Julia at one, she'd better start getting ready.

Much later that day, Catherine stared in disbelief at the piles of shopping bags on her bed. What had happened this afternoon? She had gone to help Julia buy clothes, and she had ended up with several new fall outfits for herself at the same time. She hadn't planned to make any purchases, but she had found herself looking at those enticing new clothes, and the next thing she knew…

Watching Norman nosing into the bags with his usual curiosity about anything new brought into his surroundings, she wondered what had gotten into her. She had bought several snug-fitting sweaters, a couple of flirty skirts, two form-flattering dresses, two pairs of trendy jeans and a slim-cut pair of black slacks that had made her legs look about twice as long as they were.

There wasn't a pair of khaki slacks in the lot. She had even bought a pair of high-heeled leather boots to go with the jeans and skirts. Julia had thought she'd lost her mind, of course. Catherine wasn't at all sure that she hadn't.

She supposed she could blame it on the skillful and persuasive salespeople she'd encountered. But she knew that would be unfair. The truth was, she'd been standing there among all those pretty clothes and pretty women who seemed to be having such a good time trying on and accessorizing…and here she was. The owner of a new fall wardrobe that looked very different from her usual, practical style.

Her bank account was much lighter, her closet would be more crowded and her friend thought she'd flipped out. But as she drew a bold red dress out of a bag, brushing a few stray cat hairs from it as she did so, she realized that she wasn't at all sorry.

Restless. Perhaps that was the word that best summed up Catherine's mood during the next two weeks. As the temperatures grew cooler and the days shorter, she found herself fighting a constant urge to do something different in her life.

She couldn't have explained exactly why she was suddenly dissatisfied with her usual work-and-then-home-to-her-cat routine. She didn't want to believe it had been her thirtieth birthday that had left her feeling that way. She was even less inclined to attribute this new restlessness to her encounters with Mike Clancy. But something had changed....

She had begun to wear her new clothes and to pay more attention to her hair and makeup. Not to impress anyone in particular, she assured herself repeatedly. Simply to make herself feel better.

Her coworkers seemed to notice something different, but no one said anything to her about it. Because she didn't cut back on her work hours and was as visible as ever in the lab, they probably concluded that she had simply bought some new clothes for the changing season. That in itself was hardly fodder for gossip, even though a change in fashion style was rather unexpected from her.

The graduate school where she taught and researched was part of a larger medical sciences campus that included a busy hospital facility. She didn't often eat lunch in the bustling cafeteria, generally preferring to take her lunches and eat in her office, but sometimes she stopped into the cafeteria for a sandwich or a salad. She did so on a Tuesday afternoon late in October. She'd had nothing in her apartment to bring for lunch, and since it was after 1:00 p.m., she was hungry.

The usual mix of hospital employees, medical, nursing, pharmacy and other graduate students and hospital visitors mingled through the large room, carrying trays and clattering flatware. Catherine stood in line for a chef's salad, tossed a packet of low-fat dressing on her tray, then filled a plastic tumbler with ice and raspberry-flavored tea. A moment of weakness made her add a white-chocolate-chip and macadamia-nut cookie to the tray.

Finding an empty table toward the back of the room, she slid into one of the four chairs grouped around it and arranged her lunch in front of her. She pulled a stapled sheaf of papers from the canvas bag she had carried over her shoulder. She scanned the introduction of the scientific journal article as she took the first bite of her salad.

She had almost finished her lunch when a deep voice interrupted her reading. "Good afternoon, Catherine."

She glanced up at the man who had paused by her table to greet her. "Bill. I haven't seen you around in a while. How have you been?"

"Busy," he replied with a matter-of-fact shrug. "Same as usual. And you?"

"The same. Have you eaten?" she asked politely, waving a hand toward the empty chairs at her table.

"Actually, I just finished. But I'll join you for a moment, if you don't mind."

"Please do."

"Just let me grab some coffee first. Would you like a cup?"

"No, I'm good. Thanks."

She watched as he crossed the room to the coffee urns, then carried his steaming mug to the cashier to pay. Dr. William James was a pleasant-looking cardiologist of around forty, with clear gray eyes, a nose that was just a little too long and a smile that automatically set everyone around him at ease. His sandy hair was thinning at the temples, but he was still as trim and fit as a man in his early twenties, thanks to a healthy lifestyle and a well-known passion for running.

Catherine had known him for almost a year, having met him through the course of a research project for which he had consulted with her several times. She had been able to assist him with the science behind his clinical study, and they had been on friendly terms ever since, though their encounters were rare.

"So how have you been?" he asked after settling into a seat across the table from her. "Anything new and exciting in the immunology department these days?"

Stashing her journal article in the messenger bag, she shook her head. "Not unless you count the incubator going out Monday and ruining several weeks of experiments."

He grimaced. "That sounds annoying."

"Very. Fortunately, nothing particularly important was lost, but equipment malfunctions are one of the more frustrating parts of research, especially when one just happens to be a 'control freak,' as I've been accused of on more than one occasion."

He smiled at her over the rim of his coffee cup as he took another sip. Smiling herself, Catherine swallowed the last of her cookie along with a final sip of her iced tea.

"Catherine, would you like to attend a function with me this Thursday evening?"

She almost choked on her tea in response to the out-of-the-blue invitation. Setting the tumbler down rather hastily, she said, "A, uh, function?"

Nodding a bit ruefully, he explained. "It's a retirement party for Angus McNulty. Do you know him?"

"I know who he is—neurology, right? But I've never actually met him," she added, after Bill nodded to confirm the identification.

"Nice guy, though some think he's a bit gruff. Anyway, I thought I was going to be out of town this week, but my trip was canceled at the last minute, so now I guess I have to make an appearance at this thing. It would be great if you could go with me, keep me company."

It was the first time since she had met him that Bill had shown any interest in going out with her. Nor had she even contemplated seeing him socially. She didn't know why, exactly. She had known he was single— divorced, actually—and she certainly found him pleasant enough company.

She knew Karen would urge her to accept his

invitation. Even Julia would probably approve of Bill. Catherine couldn't understand why she herself was taking so long to decide how to respond to his invitation.

"Look, if you have other plans, I understand. I know it was short notice."

Making a quick decision, she shook her head. "I'd be delighted to attend the party with you."

Hadn't she been telling herself that she needed to make some changes in her life? That she needed to get out of the predictable rut she had fallen into? Besides, this would give her a chance to wear that new red dress.

Bill seemed pleased that she had accepted, though he probably wondered about the long pause that had preceded her answer. Even after they had made arrangements and gone back to their respective jobs, Catherine wondered if she should have come up with an excuse to politely decline his invitation.

She wished she could work up a bit more enthusiasm for her first date in a pathetically long time.

Chapter Five

It had to be a strange quirk of fate that had Mike stepping out of the recently vacated apartment next to Catherine's just as she reached her door late Tuesday afternoon. Toolbox in hand, he stopped with a smile.

His dark-blond hair was mussed, tumbling onto his forehead and almost into his bright-blue eyes. He wore a gray T-shirt and soft-washed jeans with a hole in the right knee. The ultracasual garments fit his muscular body to perfection. And her pulse rate, which had been slow and steady when polished and professional

Bill had asked her out, turned suddenly rapid and erratic.

"Catherine. How are you?"

"I'm very well, thank you," she replied, grateful that her voice sounded normal, at least to her own ears.

"I guess you've been busy at work. I haven't seen you around lately."

"Yes, it's been a bit hectic. You seem to be busy, too." She nodded toward the toolbox.

"I've been doing some repairs in this apartment so the painters can come in and get it ready for the new tenant. Not to mention that all the garbage disposals in the complex seem to be breaking at once. Had any trouble with yours?"

"No, it's working fine."

"Oh. Sorry to hear that."

He was smiling as he spoke, but the quip confused her a bit. Was he implying that he would have liked an excuse to visit her apartment again? She almost told him that he didn't need an excuse to drop by anytime, but she swallowed the words for fear that they would sound too suggestive.

"How's your class going?" she asked instead, steering the conversation back into familiar territory.

"I'm still not planning a career in biological sciences, but I'm hanging in there. I've got a test Friday. I don't suppose you'd be available to quiz me Thursday evening?" he asked hopefully. "I'll spring for dinner."

She almost agreed immediately. At the last moment she remembered why she could not help him. "I'm sorry. I can't on Thursday."

"No problem," he assured her with a shrug of acceptance. "You have to work, huh?"

"No, actually I have a date." She wasn't sure why she had told him that, but she suspected she wanted him to know that he wasn't the only one with a social life.

She couldn't quite read the expression that briefly crossed his face. She hoped it wasn't surprise, since that wouldn't have been particularly flattering.

"Oh. Well, I hope you have a great time. This is just a weekly quiz, and with the study tips you've already given me, I'm sure I'll do fine."

"Maybe I could make some time—"

Mike rested a hand on her arm, just beneath the hem of her three-quarter-sleeve knit top, and shook his head, smiling faintly. "I can handle it, Catherine. I think I was just looking for an excuse to spend another pleasant couple of hours with you and Norman."

She had read about it in novels. Had heard it described in songs. Had watched it happen in movies. But she had never experienced it herself. Had never even quite believed it was real, and not just a romantic fantasy. But now— with Mike's hand on her bare arm and ripples of decidedly electric sensations running from that point of contact to somewhere deep inside her—now she believed that a simple touch could be so powerful.

"Norman and I would enjoy that," she said, and no one would have called her voice quite normal that time. There was a definite hoarse edge to it.

Mike looked at his hand on her arm for several long beats. And then his eyes rose slowly to her face. "So would I."

They stood there just like that, looking into each other's eyes for a few more moments. And then a door slammed somewhere below them, followed by a burst of laughter and conversation. The noise penetrated the silence that had fallen between them, causing them both to blink and move apart. Mike's hand fell to his side.

"I'd better go," he said. "I have a class tonight."

"And I'm sure Norman is ready for his dinner."

"I'll see you around, then."

"Yes. Good luck with your test."

"Thanks. I'll, uh, let you know how it goes."

"Yes, do that." Catherine turned abruptly and opened her door, stepping into the apartment before she could make a bigger fool of herself. What was it about Mike Clancy that turned her into such a blithering idiot?

Mike had a good reason to be in the apartment next to Catherine's Thursday evening, he assured himself. He had several minor repairs to complete before the painters and carpet layers came in to finish the apartment for its new occupant. He would have been working in that apartment even if he hadn't known Catherine was going out with someone that evening.

Whatever his reason for being in that place at that time, he walked out of the empty apartment just as Catherine and her escort stepped through her door on their way to the parking lot.

Mike's first thought was that the dude was too old for her. Too stuffy. Only then did he reluctantly concede that he looked like a nice guy with a friendly face and nice gray eyes. He supposed most people would think this man and Catherine made a very attractive couple.

As for Catherine—she looked amazing. He had only seen her in casual clothing before. The red dress she wore this evening made his breath catch hard in his chest. It was cut into a scoop at the front, and the hem fell into little points that drew his eyes down to a pair of long, slender legs. Her narrow feet were encased in strappy sandals that revealed red-painted toenails.

He found himself fighting a sudden urge to cover those pretty feet with their frivolously painted nails. Why couldn't she have worn her usual sensible shoes?

He thought she looked just a bit disconcerted upon seeing him there. And for some reason, that pleased him. "Hey, Catherine."

"Hi, Mike."

"How's Norman?"

She smiled. "He's fine. Last I saw, he was curled up asleep in my briefcase."

As if she were suddenly aware of neglecting her manners, she turned to her companion with a slight start. "Oh. Mike Clancy, this is my friend Dr. Bill James."

A doctor. Of course. Mike stuck out his hand, which he was reasonably sure was clean enough for a handshake. "Nice to meet you."

To give him credit, the man in the ultraexpensive suit didn't even hesitate to shake the hand of the guy in the tool belt and jeans.

"It's a pleasure," he said, and looked as though he meant it.

He seemed to be quite nice. There was no reason at all for Mike to dislike him. Except the fact that Dr. Bill had a hand on Catherine's back and was obviously prepared to escort her down the stairs.

"I'll see you later, Catherine," he said, making that a promise.

She nodded. "See you, Mike."

He watched as they made their way down the stairs and to a dark, expensive sedan. He was still scowling after them when the sedan had left the parking lot, passing Mike's mud-splattered pickup truck on the way out.

Catherine had attended dozens of parties like this one. Medical and science professionals standing around drinking too much and talking shop. Speeches prefaced by lame jokes, and toasts that went on for too long. Food that disappeared at a rather astonishing rate. Cell phones chiming and cameras flashing and dishes clattering. And yet the atmosphere overall was restrained and dignified.

Though he had claimed to dread the event, Bill seemed to be in his element. He worked the room like a pro, shaking hands, making jokes, exchanging bits of interdepartmental gossip. He and Catherine had several mutual acquaintances among the guests, and they introduced each other to the people only one of them knew.

Catherine noticed a few looks of surprise at seeing them together, but the surprise was quickly followed by smiles of approval. Apparently she and Bill were being seen as a suitable couple.

She liked him. He was amusing, courteous, attentive. She respected his work and admired what he had accomplished professionally. And yet, there was no electricity when he touched her. No little quivers that went down her spine when their eyes met. No schoolgirl urge to giggle when he smiled at her.

It bothered her considerably that she was so acutely aware of those things.

"These retirement parties are incredibly dull,

aren't they?" Bill asked her after a couple of hours, though he was still smiling from his recent exchange with the head of the Radiology Department.

"I'm having a very nice time," she assured him.

He chuckled. "Diplomatically spoken."

"But true." She glanced toward the busy exits. "Quite a few people seem to be leaving."

"Yes. Angus is likely to hang around telling old anecdotes for hours yet. We should probably make our escape before we're the last ones here to listen to them."

A short while later, Catherine was strapped into the soft leather passenger's seat of Bill's luxury sedan. It was a beautiful car, and probably cost three times what she had paid for her economy compact. She made what she deemed to be a decent salary, though she chose to live rather frugally and bank a tidy amount for her future. Still, she was sure Bill earned considerably more than she did, and he didn't seem to mind spending it.

Catherine couldn't care less what Bill was

worth. Having always intended to support herself, whether or not she remained single, salary had never been a criterion for her when deciding who she should date. So, if the fancy car was meant to impress, it didn't quite work that way with her.

They talked about her work during the short drive to her apartment. Bill asked questions about her research and seemed genuinely interested in her answers. Since she was more accustomed to men getting glazed looks of boredom on their faces when she talked about her work, that made a refreshing change.

He turned the car into her parking lot and negotiated the turns toward her building. "That was the apartment maintenance guy I met earlier? Mike?"

Her fingers tightened spasmodically around the purse in her lap. "Yes. Mike Clancy."

"Seems like a nice guy."

"Yes, he is."

"So you have a cat, huh? I didn't see it when I picked you up."

"Norman's a bit shy. He usually hides when the doorbell rings." Except with Mike, of course, she remembered. Norman had taken to Mike immediately, and oddly seemed to know when Mike was the one on the other side of the door.

"I see."

"Do you like cats?"

Bill shrugged. "Sure. I guess. I'm not really much of an animal person. I prefer companions who can carry on a conversation with me."

Catherine thought of the many conversations she'd had with Norman. She kept those memories to herself, since she didn't think Bill would understand. Mike, she suspected, would totally get it.

And darn it, she was doing it again. Thinking about Mike while she was out with another man.

Bill walked her to her door, then stood by while she stuck her key in the lock. She considered, then rejected asking him in for coffee. To be honest, she was ready for the evening to end, even though it wasn't particularly late.

"I have to be in the lab early tomorrow morning," she said.

He smiled faintly and nodded. "I have to get an early start myself. Thank you for going with me tonight. You made the evening much more enjoyable."

"Thank you for inviting me. I had a very nice time."

"Maybe we can do it again sometime?"

Her smile felt too bright even to her. "Maybe we can."

"Okay. Good night, Catherine."

"Good night, Bill." She turned and slipped inside her apartment, closing the door behind her.

Norman peeked out of the bedroom door to make sure she was alone. Seeing that she was, he padded out of the bedroom and wound himself around her ankles, meowing.

Catherine reached down to pick him up, heedless of the cat hairs being deposited on her dress. She could take care of that later. Right now she just wanted to snuggle her cheek against her pet's soft fur.

She'd had a perfectly nice evening. Bill had been an ideal escort, a true gentleman in the best, old-fashioned sense of the word. She was reasonably sure he would ask her out again. He seemed to have noticed that so many others considered them a good match.

She couldn't imagine why the evening had left her feeling vaguely depressed.

Catherine worked late Friday evening, returning home weary and frustrated after a day when almost everything that could go wrong had. To make it worse, gossip had spread rapidly about her accompanying Bill James to Dr. McNulty's retirement party, and quite a few of her associates had felt compelled to comment. The matchmaking had been blatant, and as a result Catherine's nerves were on edge by the end of the day.

She was hungry, but too tired to cook, so she ate a bowl of cereal and a banana for dinner, ignoring the disapproving echo of her mother's voice in her head. There were several things she should have done that evening—some laundry and other household chores, bills stacked on the desk in the bedroom she used as an office, papers to look over for the classes she taught on Mondays and Wednesdays—but those things required more energy than she had left over. Instead, she crashed in front of the television with a cup of hot tea and tried to lose herself in a crime-solving drama featuring two attractive brothers.

The first commercial break had just begun when someone knocked on the door. Snoozing in her lap, Norman raised his head with an inquiring meow.

Catherine set the cat on the sofa cushions beside her and rose. She had changed into comfortable black yoga pants and a lime-green long-sleeved T-shirt when she'd arrived home, so she was decently dressed for visitors, but she wasn't expecting anyone.

She checked the viewer in her door. Her heart gave a jump in her chest.

She opened the door. "Mike."

"Hi." Looking a little sheepish, he shifted on his feet. Along with his usual jeans and athletic shoes, he wore a thin black sweatshirt with what she assumed was a sports mascot emblazoned on the chest. "Is this a bad time?"

"No, of course not. Come in. Is something wrong?"

"No." He pushed a hand through his hair as he entered, leaving it tumbled around his forehead.

Closing the door behind him, Catherine studied his unusually somber expression. "You look so serious. I thought maybe—"

"No, everything's fine," he assured her with a quick shake of his head. "I was just having second thoughts about intruding on you like this."

"You aren't interrupting anything. Norman and I were just watching TV."

He glanced down at the cat, who sat attentively at his feet, gazing up at him as if waiting to be entertained. Mike reached down belatedly to scratch the cat's ears. "Hey, Norman. Sorry to interrupt your program."

"Can I get you anything?" Catherine offered, still uncertain of his mood. "Soda? Tea?"

"No, I'm fine." Mike straightened and pushed

his fingertips into his jeans pockets. "I just thought I'd let you know I got an A on my quiz today. The professor posted the answers after class and I only missed one out of twenty questions."

"That's great," she said with a smile. "You must be pleased."

"Yeah. It was pretty easy material this time."

"Or maybe it's just starting to seem easier to you because you've learned how to study."

He shrugged. "Could be. Anyway, you said you wanted me to let you know how it went."

"Yes, I did. Thank you." She hadn't necessarily meant that he should stop by this evening, but she supposed he was justifiably proud of his achievement. Funny thing was, he didn't look all that excited about it.

Mike sighed deeply. "I've got to come clean with you, Catherine."

She lifted an eyebrow. "You didn't really make an A?"

"No, that part was true. I got the A. But I didn't stop by tonight just to tell you about it."

"You didn't?"

"No."

"So," she prodded after another moment, "you really came tonight because…?"

"That guy you were with last night," he said, startling her again. "That doctor. Did you tell him you've been tutoring me?"

"No. Why?"

"I just thought—well, maybe he wouldn't like me spending time here. In your apartment. Alone with you."

Catherine planted her hands on her hips and looked at him in bewilderment. "Why would Bill care about that?"

"Well, you know. If you and he are—"

"We're friends," she supplied when he paused. "Colleagues. We attended a hospital function together last night. That's it."

"So you're not—"

"No. We're not."

Mike reached down to pick up Norman, who had fallen onto his back and was shamelessly begging for attention. He looked down at the cat when he spoke again, avoiding Catherine's eyes. "He seemed like a decent guy. Just your type, I would imagine."

"My type?" she repeated coolly, her hands drawing into fists on her hips.

"Well, yeah. You've both got advanced degrees. Successful careers. You've got a lot in common."

"I suppose."

"A lot more than you'd have in common with a maintenance guy who only has a high school diploma and is struggling to get a few gen ed credits at the local university."

"Surely you aren't implying that I am an educational snob when it comes to choosing my friends."

"I didn't say that," he replied just a shade too quickly.

"You certainly hinted at it." Catherine didn't lose her temper very often, but she was quite capable of expressing her displeasure when necessary. "Have I *ever* acted as though I thought less of you because you don't have a college degree?"

Mike's tone turned defensive when he

snapped back, "I don't see you going out with me, either."

"You haven't asked me to go out with you!" she retorted in exasperation.

"I—" He stopped with a funny expression on his face. "No, I guess I haven't."

"And why is that?"

"I didn't think you would say yes."

"Why wouldn't I?"

"Well…because. I'm the maintenance guy."

She sighed gustily. "You know what, Mike? I'm not the educational snob. You are."

He looked stunned by the accusation. "*I* am?"

"Exactly." She nodded in satisfaction at having so neatly turned the tables on him. "You're the one with the hang-up about our educational differences. You made it such a big deal that you wouldn't even ask if I would be interested in going out with you."

"So what would you have said if I had asked?"

She looked at him standing there, flushed and rumpled, her cat draped over his arm, and she gulped. "I would have said yes."

He studied her face as if trying to determine her sincerity. "You would?"

She nodded.

After a moment Mike grimaced. "Did this argument sound as stupid to you as it did to me?"

Her cheeks going warm, she nodded. "I'm afraid so."

Shaking his head, he set Norman on the floor. "I'm sorry. I guess I came primed for a fight."

"Why?" she asked, confused.

Taking two steps toward her, he rested his hands on her shoulders, setting off the usual cascades of reaction inside her as a result of the contact between them. "Because I'm an idiot. And because when I watched you leave with that guy yesterday, I realized that I was a fool for not having asked you sooner myself."

Now that their tempers had cooled, Catherine felt rather self-conscious. She moistened her lips as she gazed up at him. "I, um…"

"Since I've already got so much to apologize for tonight," he murmured.

And he lowered his head…slowly, his eyes

locked with hers, giving her plenty of time to stop him if she wanted to.

She didn't want to stop him. Instead she lifted her face to his.

Chapter Six

Catherine's eyes closed when Mike's mouth settled onto hers. She thought perhaps her heart stopped, as well, but then it kicked into high gear, racing so hard in her chest that she knew he had to feel it, too.

She should have expected this extreme reaction to his kiss. After all, just the feel of his hand on her arm had had a profound effect on her. But this: the feel of his solid body against hers; his muscular arms around her; the slight roughness of five o'clock shadow; his lips firm and warm against hers, moving with an easy skill that made every nerve ending in her body tingle.

This was more than she could have possibly imagined. It was more than she had ever experienced from a simple kiss—which said a great deal about the kisses that had preceded it, she thought dazedly.

He finally lifted his head, though he didn't release her. She forced her heavy eyelids upward, almost reluctant to see his expression. She was quite sure that she would be able to tell right away that the kiss had not affected Mike the way it had her. That to him, it had just been an ordinary kiss—and that he would probably be startled to learn that it had pretty much been a life-changing experience for her.

She didn't know what to think when she saw that he looked almost as dazed as she felt.

There was always the chance that she was reading him wrong, of course. Maybe he always looked as though he'd been blindsided after he kissed someone.

He cleared his throat, but his voice was just a bit rough-edged when he said, "I'm prepared to apologize, if you want—but I've got to tell you I'm not at all sorry we did that."

Her hands still rested on his chest. She flexed her fingers, savoring the tensile strength beneath his sweatshirt. "Neither am I."

His smile made her bare toes curl into the carpet. "I'm really glad to hear that. I hope you'll feel the same way after this—"

And his mouth was on hers again, the kiss deeper this time. Hungrier. Catherine wrapped her arms around his neck and molded herself into his embrace. There was no mistaking his reaction this time.

It was only a need for oxygen that finally ended this kiss. They gasped in unison, and both were breathing rapidly as they stood locked together, exploring the newness of being this close.

"This has been building for a while," Mike admitted at length, speaking softly into her ear. "For me, at least. I was attracted to you from the first time we met, and it has only gotten stronger the more time we spent together. I guess I didn't realize how strong the attraction had become until I saw you leave with that doctor last night."

"Bill is just a friend," she told him again, though she couldn't help feeling just a bit pleased by his admission of jealousy. As irrational as it might be, she was only human, and woman enough to take pleasure in having this delectable male confess his attraction to her.

"You and I have been 'just friends,' too," Mike said with a crooked smile. "But that doesn't mean I haven't wanted it to be more. Judging from the way he looked at you last night, I suspect Dr. Bill would understand."

She started to deny that, then remembered the way Bill had looked at her when he had suggested that maybe they could get together again sometime. Perhaps he *was* considering the possibility that there could be more than friendship between them.

Catherine might have contemplated pursuing that possibility herself, had she not been so obsessed with Mike. The fact that she had known Mike only six weeks while she had been acquainted with Bill for almost a year was probably a clue that there was something lacking in the chemistry between her and the cardiologist.

Mike drew a deep breath and dropped his arms to his sides. He took a quick step back from her, as though to place himself out of reach of temptation. "I'd better go."

As much as she would have liked to ask him to stay, she knew it was too soon for that. "I'm glad you came by."

His smile pushed a sexy dimple into his left cheek. "So am I. And by the way—I apologize for my bad behavior."

Though there wasn't even a hint of real regret in his voice, she returned the smile and said, "Apology accepted."

"So I'll pick you up tomorrow? Seven o'clock?"

She hadn't officially agreed to go out with him, but she supposed that was a moot point now. "I'll be ready."

"Great." He lingered a bit longer, his gaze drifting down to her mouth. And then he resolutely straightened his shoulders and moved toward the door.

Catherine stood right where she was for several

minutes after he left, reliving every moment that had passed since he'd knocked on her door. She could still feel the imprint of his arms around her, hear the echo of his heart beating wildly against her own, feel his mouth moving against hers. She lifted her fingertips to her mouth, and her lips felt warm and slightly swollen. Deliciously so.

Perhaps concerned that she had been standing there so long without moving, Norman meowed and butted his head against her ankle. Roused from her reverie, she started and looked around. Her apartment appeared exactly the same as it had earlier. The television was still playing unheeded in its cabinet, though the credits were now rolling for the program she had been watching.

Very little time had actually passed since Mike had shown up at her door, but so much had changed.

"This," she told Norman, lifting him into her arms, "could prove to be complicated."

Catherine should have expected Karen to call her Saturday morning. Karen had been out of town at a meeting in Memphis Thursday and Friday and hadn't been around to hear about Catherine's date with Bill. Catherine had known, however, that Karen would hear about it quickly and would have plenty to say about it.

Karen didn't even bother to say hello when Catherine answered the phone. "What's this I hear about you going out with Bill James?"

Catherine sighed and put down the pen she'd been using to make comments on a grad student's paper. "How was your meeting?"

"Forget that. I want to know about you and Bill. I've thought for a long time that you and Bill would make a great couple. I'd actually considered trying to set up something between you. But I guess he beat me to the punch, hmm? Did you have a good time?"

"Yes, it was very pleasant."

"Anna Vincent said you looked really good together. Everyone thought so."

"Well. Um." What was she supposed to say to that?

"So why don't you come to dinner tonight

and tell me all about it? I'll make your favorite," Karen added enticingly. "Lemon chicken."

"As good as that sounds, I can't. I have plans."

"Oh? Are you and Bill going out again?"

"No." Catherine thought about not telling her friend who she was seeing that evening, but that would be pointless. Karen would find out, and then she'd be annoyed that Catherine hadn't told her sooner. "I have a date with Mike."

"Mike?" Karen repeated in confusion. "Who's Mike?"

"You know. Mike Clancy. The guy from the restaurant?"

"The gorgeous blond?" Karen asked with a gasp.

"Um, yeah. I guess."

"When did *that* happen?"

"He asked me yesterday." As for the details, she had no intention of sharing those, even with Karen.

"Wow. You've got quite a social life going this week, don't you?"

It was a sad commentary on Catherine's usual

routines that two dates would count to Karen as a thriving "social life." Catherine managed a weak laugh. "I guess so."

"Wow," Karen said again. "Mike is really good-looking. That should be an interesting evening."

Interesting. The same word Catherine herself had used the night before. And not necessarily a good thing.

"So, anyway, do you think Bill will ask you out again?"

"I don't know. Maybe. He said he would."

"That would be great. You and Bill have so much in common. You'd make a wonderful couple." Implying, of course, that it was less likely that she and Mike were destined to be together.

"You know, Karen, I have several papers to read before Mike arrives this evening…"

"Oh. Okay, sorry. Have fun tonight, and I'll see you Monday, okay?"

"Yeah, sure. Monday." Maybe by then she would be better prepared to deal with her well-meaning but inquisitive friend.

* * *

Mike was running behind, but only by twenty minutes, so he wasn't too worried about it. He had gotten tied up with a repair project in the complex, and then an old baseball buddy had called and time, as it so often did, had somehow slipped away from him.

Remembering how pleased she had seemed the last time, he almost brought flowers again. But that would have made him even later, and besides, he didn't like to repeat himself.

His steps were quick with anticipation as he approached her apartment. No backpack this time, he thought in satisfaction. The only biology they would be studying tonight was their own.

Who would have thought quiet, serious, brainy Dr. Catherine Travis would turn him into six feet of quivering jelly with only a kiss? And yet somehow he had known from the first time he'd met her that there was more to her than she let people see.

He stopped at her door, running his hands down the front of his khaki slacks as if to dry palms damp with nerves. Three days before the end of October, the air was just a little chilly, so he'd worn a thin brown-and-buff patterned sweater over a khaki-colored T-shirt. Hardly an expensive tailored suit, like the one Dr. Bill had worn the other night, but he thought he looked pretty good.

Picturing the way Catherine had looked in her sleek red dress, he gulped, wondering if *pretty good* was adequate tonight. They hadn't discussed plans for the evening. What if she was expecting a fancy outing at a jacket-and-tie place where he would have to pay for dinner on the credit-card installment plan?

It wasn't like him to be so uncertain at the beginning of a date. Shaking his head in impatience, he tapped on Catherine's door.

She opened it immediately, and he was relieved to see that, while she looked very nice, she had dressed no more formally than he had. She wore a forest-green sweater with a vee neckline and three-quarter-length cuffed sleeves, tan slacks and heeled brown leather boots that added another couple of inches to her five-foot-seven frame. Gold hoops dangled from her ears, drawing his gaze to her earlobes and making him wonder if she liked having them nibbled.

Whoa, buddy. A little too early for that line of thought, he chided himself.

"You look great," he said.

Her smile looked a little strained around the edges. "I thought maybe something had gone wrong."

"Why would you?"

She shook her head. "I guess you were just running late again?"

"Oh, that." He shrugged apologetically. "Yeah, sorry. I got held up by a call from an old friend."

"Would you like to come in for a few minutes before we leave?"

"Yeah. Actually, I bought a gift."

She closed the door behind him. "You didn't have to do that."

"Oh, it's not for you." He pulled a white

rabbit-hair toy mouse from his pocket. "This is for Norman."

This time her smile was completely genuine. "He'll like that."

Mike tossed the toy on the floor in front of the cat. Norman approached the new item cautiously, sniffed it, then picked it up by the tail and tossed it in the air. When it landed, he pounced on it with a meow of victory. He looked prepared to spend the next half hour happily battling the hapless mouse.

"That was nice of you," Catherine said warmly, apparently having forgotten his tardiness now. "On behalf of Norman, thank you."

"Norman is very welcome." Downright proud of himself, Mike made a vow to be punctual next time he had plans with Catherine. Because he did intend for there to be a next time. Of course, he had made promises to himself about punctuality before, and he still hadn't gotten much better at it. But for Catherine's sake he would try harder.

"Can I get you anything?" she asked.

"No, thanks. Are you ready to go?"

"Of course. But you never told me where we're going," she reminded him, picking up her purse.

He opened the door for her. "I thought we would just wing it. That's always more fun than planning all the details, don't you think?"

She stepped out into the night, which was already dark at six-thirty now that fall had settled in to stay. The many security lights posted around the upscale complex spread a bright, if somewhat harsh glow over the parked cars and the closed-for-the-season swimming pool in the center of the compound. Lights burned in many of the apartment windows and in the large pool house, which also contained the workout room. Through the windows of that structure, they could see people making use of the treadmills and stair climbers and stationary bikes. Other residents moved through the parking lot toward their cars, headed out for Saturday-evening activities or toward their apartments.

Catherine paused at the passenger's door of

Mike's truck. "I tend to be a planner," she confessed. "Calendars and lists and organizers. I guess it's a side effect of my work, which has to be planned and timed very precisely."

He opened the door for her. "Tonight we're throwing away the lists and the organizer."

She shot a look upward at him, and he thought that maybe there was just a hint of apprehension in her eyes. Giving her a trust-me smile, he closed the door of the pickup he had washed and vacuumed just for this outing and made a promise to himself that she wouldn't miss her organizer at all tonight.

Catherine was beginning to believe that Mike Clancy was the most impulsive man she had ever met. Maybe it was because she was used to being around scientists and academics, who pretty much breathed according to their rigid schedules, but she wasn't accustomed to spending an entire evening just acting on whims.

Mike didn't even have a restaurant in mind when they left the apartment complex. Instead he asked, "What kind of food are you in the mood for tonight? Steak? Seafood? Italian?"

Assuming he wouldn't have asked if he wasn't interested in what she would like, she replied, "Sushi sounds pretty good."

"Sushi?" He looked at her as if expecting her to admit that she was only joking. "Really?"

"Well, yes. But if you don't care for it—"

"No, I can find you some sushi. No problem."

And he took her straight to an all-you-can-eat Chinese buffet that offered a few California rolls on one of the long buffet tables. Having expected him to select one of the excellent sushi restaurants in the area—or at least one of the Japanese restaurants—Catherine was a bit surprised, but she decided that this was his way of compromising. Obviously, sushi wasn't one of his favorite dishes.

The atmosphere was rather noisy, and the buffet tables were crowded with adults and children who had apparently taken the "all you can eat" invitation as a challenge. She placed some steamed rice, beef with vegetables and a couple of California rolls on her plate, then carried it to the booth where she and Mike had been seated. Mike joined her a short while later, his own plate piled so high that the egg roll balanced on top teetered precariously. She noticed that most of his food selections were fried, and that he was most definitely a carnivore.

"Great place, isn't it?" he asked happily. "Something for everyone."

"It looks good," she replied, stabbing her fork into a thin slice of beef. Privately she thought that he either had a phenomenal metabolism or he didn't eat this way very often. Otherwise he wouldn't still be so slim.

Once again she needn't have worried about making conversation during dinner. Mike talked enough for both of them. While somehow making impressive inroads into his plate of food, he chatted nonstop about a dizzying array of topics. He pelted her with questions and seemed genuinely interested in her answers, but unlike Bill he was more interested in her past and her personal life than her work.

He wanted to know her tastes in music and movies, but he seemed to have little interest in books or politics. He admitted to a passion for sports, in addition to being unhealthily addicted to television and video games. She responded that she occasionally watched a tennis match on TV and had always thought she might like to learn golf, but she hadn't played a video game since trying a few arcade classics in college. Even then she had been spectacularly bad at them.

He talked about his parents, a retired plumber and a former elementary school teacher. And his four sisters, Gretchen, Amy, Charlotte—also known as Charlie—and Laurie, who ranged in age from thirty-three to twenty-nine. Gretchen and Amy were married and had two children apiece—boys for Gretchen, girls for Amy—so Mike was an uncle, a role he apparently enjoyed greatly. Catherine talked about being an only child and how she had occasionally wished for siblings, especially a sister.

She and Mike had very little in common,

actually. But it surprised her how easy it was to talk with him.

He plowed through a plate of assorted desserts while she ate a few small pastries. Afterward, they stood at a cash register where he insisted on paying for both of them. They walked through an entryway filled with vending machines holding gum, candy and small toys, and then through the busy parking lot to his truck.

"What do you want to do now?" Mike asked as he started the engine. "It's too early to call it a night."

"Oh, I…um…" She didn't have a clue. "What would *you* like to do?"

He flashed her a grin. "This could go on a while. Let's just cruise and see what grabs us, okay?"

Cruise and see what grabbed them? How odd. "Okay. Sure."

He tuned into a rock station on his radio, then talked above the pounding music as he drove in a seemingly aimless pattern around the city streets. He talked about the weather, giving even that prosaic subject a personal twist.

"Feels good tonight. Just a little cool. It's been pretty warm for late October, hasn't it? I used to hate it when it was too warm at Halloween. There's nothing worse than sweating inside a heavy costume when you're out trick-or-treating. Of course, it wasn't much better when it was unseasonably cold, and my mom made me wear a coat over my costume—which I ditched as soon as I was out of her sight, of course."

"I never went trick-or-treating, but growing up mostly in Florida, I was accustomed to choosing lightweight costumes on the few occasions when I dressed up for parties."

Mike went suddenly silent, and when she glanced at him, she noticed that he wore what could only be described as a horrified expression. "You never went trick-or-treating?"

"No. I didn't have siblings to go with me. And my parents considered the practice frivolous and rather dangerous. Mother said it was 'distasteful' to go door-to-door, demanding treats from people, only to then overindulge in unhealthy sweets."

Mike seemed too dismayed to respond.

Laughing a little, she touched his arm in a gesture that was almost reassuring. "Don't start thinking I had a deprived or unhappy childhood. It isn't true. I was completely indulged. We traveled a lot and spent a great deal of happy time together. My parents weren't into Santa Claus and the Easter Bunny and some other traditional childhood fantasies, but they made sure I had wonderful birthdays and Christmases and summer vacations."

"I'm glad you had a happy childhood. But still—no trick-or-treating." He shook his head.

She laughed again. "You make it sound as though I was regularly beaten. Trust me, Mike, I don't feel in the least deprived."

He glanced her way with a smile. "I like hearing you laugh. Have you ever been to a haunted house?"

"I, um—" The unexpectedly rattling compliment, followed by the totally unrelated question, made her blink. "A haunted house? You mean, a *real* haunted house? Because as a scientist, I don't believe they really—"

"Not a real haunted house," he broke in quickly. "Though my sister Laurie could tell you a few hair-raising stories about a weekend she spent in a cottage in the Ozarks. But I was talking about one of the haunted houses that are put on every year by various charities."

"Oh. That. No, I've never been to one, though I've heard them advertised quite a bit on the car radio lately."

He promptly turned left at the next intersection. "This is something that can be remedied immediately."

"Oh, I—"

"Trust me," he said with another bright grin that didn't do a thing to reassure her. "This will be fun."

Chapter Seven

Mike drove to an old building on the outskirts of downtown that had been taken over by a local community theater group for the holiday. Overflow parking was provided in the lot of a vacant former business across the street, and Mike found an empty space fairly quickly, though the lot was almost full.

A long line of customers stood in line at the ticket window. The crowd was noisy, mostly young, ethnically diverse. Catherine caught the distinct odor of alcohol from some of the rowdier groups. Some of the visitors had come in costume, but they didn't unnerve her as much as the ones who seemed to dress disturbingly as a fashion statement.

She was definitely out of her comfort zone here, she reflected as she moved just a bit closer to Mike.

Smiling, he draped an arm casually around her shoulders. "It will be fun," he repeated.

With every nerve ending in her body tingling in response to his arm around her, she could only try to smile.

They waited quite some time, and Catherine tried not to eavesdrop too blatantly on the conversations going on around them. It wasn't easy, since most of them were carried on in fairly loud voices.

A group of four teenage girls stood in front of them, all dressed to attract male attention, all seemingly giggling into cell phones that looked permanently attached to their ears rather than talking to each other. Or maybe they were talking to each other and their cell phone friends at the same time, Catherine mused, since they seemed to be babbling without stopping to breathe.

A young couple behind her indulged in occasional demonstrations of passion that would have been more appropriate in the back seat of their car. Two men in their late twenties to early thirties were eyeing the teenage girls and talking too loudly about topics presumably chosen to make them sound young and "cool," but in Catherine's opinion only made them rather pathetic. But what did she know? Scientists weren't exactly known for their "coolness" quotients.

Speaking of cool…she glanced up at Mike again. She needed to remind herself again why she was here. The encouraging smile he aimed at her provided a partial explanation.

Eventually, of course, they arrived at the head of the line. Catherine was less than thrilled to discover that the teenage girls and the groping couple would be included in their tour group. An exotic-looking young woman in a long, hooded black robe and very pale foundation paired with smoky, dark eye shadow and bloodred lipstick introduced herself as their guide, "Almyra."

Stifling a sigh, Catherine tried to work up some enthusiasm for what was to come. She found some encouragement in reminding herself that she loved community theater and believed very strongly in supporting local artists. Even if she found the next few minutes boring or silly, that should make it more worthwhile for her.

She just hoped the teenagers around them wouldn't try to outscream each other, leaving her with a pounding headache when this was over.

"Are you okay, Catherine? You're still a little pale."

She took another deep swallow of margarita and attempted a smile. "I'm fine. Really."

"Glad to hear it." Mike had been doing a pretty fair job of stifling a grin ever since they had left the haunted house a half hour earlier. As if sensing that she could use a little liquid reinforcement, he had brought her straight to a popular music bar. The place was crowded and noisy and rather smoky, but at least no gruesome monsters lurked beneath the tables, ready to leap out at her and scare the stuffing out of her.

The repressed smile tugged at the corners of Mike's mouth. "So now you can say that you have finally visited a haunted house."

She nodded and took another drink.

A quick laugh escaped him. "I have to admit you handled it well. Those silly girls with us were screaming and carrying on all the way through the place, while you didn't make a peep. I thought you were just sort of bored by it all—until we got back outside and I saw that you were almost as white as the ghosts who howled at us inside."

"It was a little…unnerving in there," she admitted, suppressing a shudder. It had been so dark, with creepy music and sound effects and dry-ice fog drifting around them. And even though she had known the assorted ghosts and goblins had all been volunteers in gory latex costumes, she had still almost jumped out of her boots every time one of them popped out of the darkness and shrieked at her.

"Well, yeah. That was the point. Sometimes it's kind of fun to be scared, you know? That's why horror movies and roller coasters are so popular."

"I hate horror movies. And you would have to hold a gun to my temple to get me on a roller coaster."

"So you didn't have any fun at the haunted house?"

She was being ungracious, she realized abruptly. Mike had paid for her ticket, thought he was providing her with an experience she had missed in her youth, and all she had done was disparage the experience.

"It was interesting," she conceded in an attempt at diplomacy. "Something I had never done before."

She was tempted to add that she would have been perfectly content to live out the remainder of her life without ever experiencing that particular pleasure, but that would have been discourteous again.

"It was pretty funny when that vampire dude swooped down from the ceiling, wasn't it? I thought that little blonde in our tour group was going to wet her pants."

Because she had come dangerously close to that reaction herself, Catherine could only smile weakly and say, "Yes. That was… amusing."

And to think that she had always taken such pride in her honesty.

"So I guess this means you don't want to go to the horror movie marathon with me Halloween night?"

"Gee, I would—but I'm washing my cat that night."

Her drawled joke seemed to please him. Laughing, he said, "Could I talk you into doing that little chore some other time and going to a party with me, instead?"

"A party?"

He nodded. "My sister Laurie's throwing a party and she pretty much expects me to be there. I'd really like it if you would go with me."

"Is it a costume party?"

"Well, sure. It's Halloween."

She bit her lower lip for a moment before asking, "What are you going to wear?"

He shrugged. "I haven't really thought much about it yet. Last year I went as a handheld video game."

Intrigued despite herself, she asked, "How did you manage that?"

"Oh, you know. Big fake control buttons surrounding a fake screen painted on a sweatshirt. I drew video game characters on the screen, and taped a couple of big fake batteries to my back. Clipped a little CD player loaded with video game sounds to my belt. Covered my head with one of those sheer black hoods you can see through from the inside but not so much from the outside. It turned out pretty good—though everyone thought it was real funny to keep poking my 'buttons.' I ended up with a few bruises on my ribs by the end of the evening."

"It sounds very creative. I've never been very clever at that sort of thing."

He shrugged. "Heck, you can wear a tiara and call yourself a princess. It isn't a contest."

She wasn't good at parties. Business functions such as the one she had attended with Bill, sure. She was used to those. But a costume party with strangers—one of whom was the stunning and vivacious redhead who had drawn so much attention at the restaurant? Totally different story.

Every instinct told her she would be more comfortable declining the invitation. But wasn't *comfortable* a word she had recently begun to chafe against? Hadn't she become increasingly dissatisfied with her predictable ruts and vowed to make some changes, even if it meant challenging herself occasionally?

And did she really want to turn down a chance to spend another evening with Mike?

"Okay," she said after drawing a deep breath. "It could be fun."

"Trust me," he said with a smile, picking up his mug of beer. "It will be great."

Which was pretty much what he had said about the haunted house experience, she couldn't help remembering.

"Just promise me no one at the party will

leap down at me from the ceiling and try to suck my blood."

He grinned even more broadly. "I'm pretty sure none of the other party guests will try anything like that. As for me—well, I'll try to restrain myself, but you do have a very tempting neck."

She lifted a hand automatically to her throat, thinking that maybe she should have worn a turtleneck tonight.

They spent quite a while in the River Market district, a revitalized section of downtown Little Rock that ran alongside the Arkansas River. Lined with bars, restaurants and music venues, shops, art galleries and museums, including the Clinton Presidential Center, and with a large sports-and-concert arena on the North Little Rock side of the river, the area had become a popular destination for tourists in the daytime and local barhoppers and music lovers in the evenings.

Catherine hadn't spent much time there herself except during the summer months when she often dropped by early on Saturday mornings for fresh produce from the bustling farmer's market. Still, she enjoyed her evening there with Mike.

Mike walked her to the door when he finally took her home. "I had a great time here with you this evening. Sorry about scaring you so badly in the haunted house."

"I wasn't actually scared," she said, feeling the need to defend herself. "I knew I was in no danger. As I said, it was simply an unnerving experience."

"Then I'm sorry you were unnerved."

"And I'm sorry I didn't enjoy it more," she said with a sigh. "I know you expected to have more fun there. I didn't mean to throw a wet blanket on your evening."

"Hey, don't apologize. So haunted houses and horror movies aren't your thing. No big deal."

She was glad he didn't seem to be offended by her lack of enthusiasm for his choice of entertainment. And she hoped the Halloween party wouldn't turn out to be another event that they would have to write off as "not her thing." She couldn't exactly say she was looking forward to it, since it made her vaguely uncomfortable to think about it. But she wasn't actively dreading it, either. After all, she would be attending with Mike.

"Look at it this way," Mike advised with a grin. "October's almost over—and Halloween with it. The next set of holidays are much more peaceful."

She didn't really expect to still be seeing Mike socially when the next set of holidays rolled around, of course. As different as they were—and this evening had been full of signs pointing to that conclusion—it was highly unlikely that anything long-term would develop between them. But in the meantime, she might as well take advantage of the opportunity to enliven her dull life with a few new experiences.

She put her hand on the doorknob. "Norman's probably wondering where I am."

She wouldn't ask him in. It was entirely too soon to be sending signals she wasn't ready to follow up on.

His smile never wavered, so maybe he hadn't expected an invitation. "Maybe I'll talk to you tomorrow?"

"You have my cell phone number if I'm not home."

"Oh? Do you have plans?" he asked casually.

"I'll be in the lab most of the day."

"On a Sunday?"

She shrugged. "Experiments don't run by a regular calendar."

"But you can take calls?"

"Sure. If it's a bad time, I'll say so."

"Okay. So I'll call."

"Good night, Mike. Thank you again for a very nice evening."

He stood close enough that she could almost feel the warmth radiating from him. "Not including the haunted house, of course."

She laughed weakly. "Let's just say I had a very interesting time. For the most part."

"Very tactful." He lowered his head to brush his mouth lightly over hers. "Good night, Catherine."

After she closed her apartment door behind him, she wondered if that wholly unsatisfying kiss had been due to gentlemanly restraint—or if he had deliberately left her wanting more. She suspected the latter. And it had most definitely worked.

Catherine had just set two six-well plates in the incubator in her lab Sunday afternoon when her cell phone rang. Her heart beating a bit more quickly, she answered it without thinking to check the caller ID. "Hello?"

"Catherine, hi. It's Bill. Is this a bad time?"

Pushing aside her instinctive disappointment, she spoke lightly. "No. I have a few minutes to talk. How are you?"

"Fine, thank you. And you?"

She assured him that she was well. Only then did he bring up a subject she had hoped to avoid. "I had such a nice time with you the other night. I was hoping we could get together again. There's a Halloween party at my country club. Would you do me the honor of going with me?

We don't have to go to a lot of trouble for costumes—we can just wear our lab coats and call ourselves a pair of mad scientists."

"Thank you for asking, Bill, but I already have plans for that evening." It felt strange to have two invitations to parties on the same night. Hardly typical for her.

"I see." He didn't even try to hide his disappointment. "I shouldn't have waited so late to ask, I suppose."

Had he asked before Mike, would she have accepted? She couldn't think of any reason why she would have turned him down, but still she was vaguely relieved that she'd had a valid excuse to decline.

"Some other time then?" he asked, injecting more cheer into his voice.

"Yes, of course."

She wondered after they disconnected if he really would ask again. And she wondered what she would say if he did and she had no other plans to use as an excuse next time.

* * *

"So who is this girl you're bringing to my party?" Laurie Clancy demanded of her brother as they sat in their parents' wood-paneled den Sunday afternoon after lunch. A football game played on their dad's cherished big-screen TV, but Laurie was more interested in her brother's social life than in the game.

"She isn't a 'girl,'" Mike corrected, reaching into a bowl for a handful of popcorn. "She's a medical researcher. She has a Ph.D. and everything."

"You're dating a scientist?" his sister Charlie demanded, sitting bolt upright in the big recliner on the other side of the den. "You?"

Mike was hardly flattered by her obvious skepticism. "Yes, I'm seeing a scientist. At least, I've only been out with her once, but I've known her a few weeks."

"Did you meet her at school, honey?" his mother, Alice, asked from her rocker, where she was crocheting a green-and-red Christmas afghan. A petite bundle of nervous energy, Alice was always making something, most of which she donated to hospitals and nursing homes through her church activities.

"No, she lives in my apartment complex. I've done some repairs for her a couple of times."

"Is she pretty?" his father, Mick, asked without looking away from the television screen. The overhead lights reflected off the bald spot in the middle of his faded red hair, and his weathered face showed little interest in the conversation despite his question.

"Daddy. That isn't important," Laurie complained with the confidence of a woman who had no doubt of her own beauty. "It's her mind that matters, not her appearance."

"She's pretty, Dad," Mike assured him. "*And* she's brilliant," he added for Laurie's benefit.

Then, because Charlie was a nut for animals, he added, "She has a cat named Norman."

"I can see why she would like the cat," Charlie answered dryly, running a hand through the red hair that she kept cut in short curls. "But what does she see in *you?*"

Laurie laughed. Alice looked up from her crocheting with a frown on the face that was still hardly lined at all beneath her stylishly tousled cap of slightly graying blond hair. "That wasn't very nice. Why wouldn't she be interested in your brother?"

Rather than answering, Charlie asked, "How old is she? I mean, she already has her doctorate, so she must be at least your age, right?"

"She got her degrees early, I guess. She just turned thirty."

Charlie frowned. "Thirty?"

"Right. Your age," he shot back pointedly. "And only a year, almost to the day, older than Laurie."

Since he and Laurie were only ten months apart, he didn't think the age gap was at all significant. What was a couple of years, after all?

"I was sort of hoping you would hit it off with Paula McDermott's younger sister, Erin, at my party," Laurie complained. "I met her at Paula's wedding shower last week, and I invited her to my party because she seemed like someone you'd like. Erin's twenty-four, and really cute.

She's just back in town after living in St. Louis for a couple of years. She's a personal trainer at Silver's Gym, and she likes a lot of the things you do. You know, sports and outdoorsy stuff. As soon as I met her, I thought, 'Here's someone who would be a really great match for Mike.'"

This time it was Mike who scowled. "You didn't tell me you were going to try to fix me up at your party. You said I could bring someone if I wanted."

"Well, yeah, but you said you weren't seeing anyone right now and you would probably just come stag," she shot back. "And it isn't really a 'fix up.' There will be quite a few unattached people there. I just thought you'd like Erin, that's all."

Mike was well accustomed to the matchmaking efforts of all his sisters, especially the two married ones, who wouldn't be satisfied until everyone they knew had a spouse, children and a house in the 'burbs. For a while the older two had concentrated on Charlie and Laurie, but now Charlie was involved with a firefighter and Laurie was seeing a local television meteorologist, so everyone's attention had turned to Mike.

"I'm sure she's very nice. And I'm sure there will be several single guys at your party for her to meet. But I'm seeing Catherine right now, so—"

"You're 'seeing' her?" Charlie broke in quizzically. "I thought you said you'd only known her for a few weeks and you've only been out with her once."

"Okay, I've just started seeing her," he admitted a bit defensively. "The point is, I don't need y'all to find dates for me. I'm perfectly capable of handling that myself."

"You haven't done such a great job of that so far," Laurie muttered.

For some reason, his sisters had never particularly approved of anyone he had dated. Only a couple of times had he been involved in real relationships, and he had never gotten to the point of actually considering marriage with anyone he had dated. Still, his sisters had found fault with each of the women he'd brought into their lives for however long the affairs had lasted. As avid as they all seemed to be to see him seriously committed, not a one of them seemed to trust his judgment when it came to choosing his own mate.

When he had complained about that to his mother, she had merely smiled and explained that it was because he was the youngest and his sisters had gotten into the habit of looking out for him. They all adored him, she reminded him, and it was hard for them to believe anyone was quite good enough for their little brother. And besides, she had added with gentle candor, it wasn't as if he had the greatest track record with that sort of thing.

So, okay, maybe some of his past relationships had been...spectacularly unsuccessful. And maybe a couple of the breakups had been...well, train wrecks. But past history aside, he wished they would give him a little more credit when it came to his personal life.

"You'll see," he told Laurie, making sure that Charlie heard him, as well. "You'll like Catherine. She's smart and successful and interesting. The type of competent, independent woman you all admire so much. The kind you all *are*, for that matter. I bet you're going to have a hard time finding *anything* to criticize about this one."

"We'll see," Laurie murmured.

Mike hoped he hadn't made it sound like a challenge.

Chapter Eight

Catherine came very close to calling Mike and telling him that something had come up, preventing her from attending the Halloween party with him. Only the awareness of how rude that would be kept her from picking up the phone.

She wondered if panic attacks were going to be a regular thing when it came to going out with him. Or if there would be any more reason to worry about that sort of thing after tonight. Funny how they could talk so easily over the phone or during his studying, but their tastes in entertainment were so radically different.

She checked her appearance one more time in her bedroom mirror. It wasn't as if she had anything else to do, except pace and second-guess her acceptance of this costume-party invitation. Mike was late. Again. At least this time he had called to apologize and let her know he'd been detained.

He wouldn't tell her what he had selected as a costume. She still wasn't sure she liked her own choice. She couldn't help thinking that it wasn't particularly original, the idea having been inspired by their guide at the community theater haunted house.

Her dress was black and formfitting, the hem falling halfway down her calves, the neckline dipping halfway to her navel. Well, maybe not quite that far, she thought, tugging self-consciously at it, but deeper than she usually wore. The oversize, silver bat-shaped pendant she wore on a black leather cord filled in some of the space, but still left more bare skin than she was accustomed to showing.

Long sleeves belled from her elbows to flutter

around the tops of her hands, on which she sported half a dozen cheap, gaudy rings. She had painted her fingernails a dark, almost black purple. She wore black hose, black shoes with ankle straps and very high heels, and dangling silver bat-shaped earrings. She'd forgone the obvious peaked hat, instead slicking back her brown hair with a dollop of gel and pinning a black silk rose just above her right ear.

Her foundation was light, her brown eyes smudged with dark-purple shadow and veiled by a heavy coat of black mascara. She wore a glittery blackish-purple shade on her lips.

She felt like an idiot. An imposter. What had she been thinking to go for sexy and mysterious? She should have just stolen Bill's idea and worn a lab coat and some nerdy plastic glasses or something. Nerd she could do. Seductress was pretty much out of her range.

Maybe there was still time to change. For all she knew, it could be another half hour before Mike arrived. She had a couple of clean lab coats in the closet....

The doorbell rang just as she reached automatically for her makeup remover.

Norman appeared in the bedroom doorway and meowed to announce her visitor. She thought he eyed her oddly when she moved away from the mirror toward him.

"Don't mock me," she warned him, "or I'll make you go to this stupid party as my familiar."

He twitched his tail as if daring her to try.

Perhaps she and Mike had been on the same mental wavelength, she thought when she opened her door. He wore unrelieved black. Silky black shirt, buttoned to the throat. Black slacks that fit him like a caress. Black boots. A long, purple-lined black cape that fell almost to his ankles. A ring with a big, bloodred stone on his right hand.

Gel darkened his swept-back blond hair, which made such a striking contrast to his dark clothing. Interestingly, a new scar had appeared on his face, running from the corner of his right eye down to his jaw. Looking as though it had been there for years, the scar added a touch of danger and mystery to his pretty-boy face.

He smiled at her, and she noticed something different about his teeth. The canines were definitely longer and sharper. They, too, looked startlingly real.

"You look amazing," he told her, his voice deep and a little startled. "Absolutely stunning."

The blush that warmed her cheeks didn't exactly match the coolly sophisticated image she had tried to capture with her costume. "Thank you. You look very dashing yourself."

Making a face that twisted his newly acquired scar into a classic, sardonic expression, he admitted, "Between work and classes, I didn't have much time to come up with anything clever this year. I borrowed the cape from a drama-major friend who played Dracula in a play last semester."

"The scar is an interesting touch."

"Same friend's stage makeup kit."

"It's very effective." She couldn't seem to keep her eyes from following the path of that fake scar to his lips. Even with the eerie, pointed teeth, he had the most beautiful mouth of any man she had ever known. Or maybe she had just never noticed any of those other men's mouths.

Mike reached out to trace a fingertip from her jaw down her throat to the bat pendant that hung just above her cleavage. A tiny shiver trailed behind his touch. She held her breath as she waited to see if his finger would move any lower.

But he merely toyed for a moment with the pendant as his gaze held hers. "I suppose it would ruin your lipstick if I kissed you right now?"

Her smile felt shaky. She wanted to tell him to hell with the lipstick, but she said, instead, "Yes. Not to mention that you'd get it on your face."

"It might be worth it," he murmured.

She placed a hand on his chest, resisting the urge to curl her fingers into his silky shirt and draw him closer. "Whoa, there, Vlad. We have a party to get to. And we're already late."

He laughed at the ironic nickname, flashing his fake teeth and easing the sudden tension between them, if only a little. "Okay, Elvira. Let's go. Before I decide to find out just how good that pretty neck of yours tastes."

She absolutely had to stop this silly blushing, Catherine told herself sternly, turning her head to try to conceal her warm cheeks from Mike. She was too old for such nonsense, and it hardly fit her costume. But just thinking about him nibbling on her neck made her go warm all over again, much to her despair.

Mike couldn't get over the way Catherine looked. Yeah, sure, he'd always thought she was attractive. He'd spent a lot of time thinking about the way she'd looked in that red dress the night she'd gone out with Dr. Bill. He even liked the casual clothes she wore on a day-to-day basis, and the way she made simple camp shirts and khakis look oddly elegant.

But tonight…tonight she took his breath away.

The black dress fit her like a second skin, gliding against her body when she moved. The skirt flirted with her legs, drawing his attention once again to the length and shape of them. The neckline dipped just low enough to send his imagination into overdrive. Her glittering dark lipstick almost begged him to take a leisurely taste. Even the damned flower in her hair made him hot.

She brushed lightly against him when he helped her into his truck, and he caught a scent of something spicy and exotic. He could imagine her dabbing the perfume lightly behind her ears. On her wrists. Perhaps between her breasts. He drew his cloak a bit more snugly around him as he rounded the front of the truck, thinking that maybe the concealing garment was going to come in handy tonight, after all.

He slid behind the wheel and fastened his seat belt, glancing at Catherine as she snapped her own. Funny how her appearance tonight made her look so much more distant. Unobtainable.

He didn't really think of her as a scientist with a Ph.D. and all, when she wore her usual clothes, even though that was her work uniform, in a way. How ironic was it that what should have been a frivolous Halloween costume would do the very opposite? Okay, so maybe she looked like a vampire, but he was very aware that she was *Dr.* Vampira.

His sisters would surely laugh at him if they could hear him thinking such crazy things. And heaven only knew what Catherine herself would think.

Maybe his fake teeth were too tight.

The party was being held in the clubhouse of Laurie's apartment complex, which wasn't far from the one where Catherine and Mike lived. Mike had to drive carefully to get there, mindful of the groups of costumed trick-or-treaters being escorted around the residential area by parents in slow-moving vehicles.

The clubhouse was spacious, with high ceilings, glittering chandeliers, a stone floor, scattered couches and small bistro-style tables and a kitchen with a large serving bar. Laurie must have reserved the room a long time ago for this occasion, Catherine mused, knowing how popular the clubhouse at her own complex was.

There were, perhaps, forty people mingling in the room. Maybe more. The music was on the loud side and prerecorded, piped in through unseen speakers. Simple Halloween decorations were scattered around the room, just enough to convey the reason for the party without going overboard. Costumes ranged from simple to elaborate, from traditional to rather perplexing—such as the guy wrapped in aluminum foil with kitchen utensils taped to various body parts. Catherine had no idea what he was trying to be.

From everything he had said about them, Catherine expected to like Mike's sisters. He was obviously crazy about them, in a long-suffering, younger brother way. He had talked about them teasing him and overindulging him and being there for him when he needed them. He had assured her that he was confident they would like her. Which made it all the more jarring when she got the distinct impression that they were fully prepared to dislike her from the beginning.

Two of the four sisters were at the party, and both descended on them as soon as they entered, as if they'd been waiting for their brother to show up. Apparently, the married sisters were spending Halloween evening with their children.

Laurie was dressed as a fairy, her stunningly perfect body draped in white gauze, small silver wings attached to her shoulders. Everything about her twinkled—the dress, the wings, her rhinestone sandals. Glitter dusted her exposed skin—of which there was rather a lot—and she wore sparkly eye shadow and lipstick. There were even rhinestones scattered in the mass of red hair that fell almost to her waist.

If Karen and Julia had thought Laurie was gorgeous in the restaurant, they should see her now, Catherine thought.

Charlie was almost as beautiful as her younger sister, though in perhaps a less obvious sort of way. Her hair was a mop of red curls, her face slightly more gamine than Laurie's classic features. She had dressed as Peter Pan, and her escort as Captain Hook, though his broad, tanned face was much too genial and approachable to play the villain properly.

Mike greeted them, then made the introductions. "Catherine, these are my sisters, Laurie and Charlie Clancy, and Charlie's friend Drew Conroy. Everyone, this is Dr. Catherine Travis."

"Nice to meet you, Dr. Travis," Drew said immediately, his voice a deep, country drawl. "You any kin to the Travises from Malvern? I went to school with some Travises there."

"Please call me Catherine. And no, my family isn't from Arkansas. I moved here a couple of years ago to accept a job with the medical sciences school."

"My brother told us you're a medical researcher," Laurie said.

Catherine nodded. "I'm an associate professor in the immunology department."

"Where did you study?" Charlie asked, her tone that of a person who felt obliged to ask polite questions.

"I earned my undergraduate degree at Vanderbilt, and my doctorate at Harvard, then did postdoctoral work at Johns Hopkins."

"Harvard?" Mike turned to Catherine in surprise. "You never told me that."

"You never asked," she replied gently. As

interested as he had been in hearing about her childhood, he hadn't asked many questions about her higher education. She had assumed that he'd been a bit uncomfortable comparing their educational experiences after high school. She had mentioned to him that she'd lived in Boston for a few years, but she supposed he hadn't put the clues together.

"No, I guess I didn't."

"Harvard to Little Rock?" Laurie asked, lifting one rhinestone-enhanced eyebrow. "That must have been quite a transition for you."

Catherine held on tightly to her patience in the face of what felt increasingly like an inquisition. "I grew up primarily in Texas and Florida and attended three years of college in Tennessee. I'm comfortable in the South. I was offered several nice benefits here, so I accepted, and I haven't regretted my decision."

"Okay if Catherine and I get a drink now, or do you want to know her shoe size first?" Mike asked his sisters ironically.

"Seven and a half," Catherine said, turning to

him with a slightly strained smile. "And I would love a drink."

He slipped an arm around her waist and turned with her toward the bar. "Come on, Vampira, I'll try to find you a nice glass of blood. See you guys later."

"Don't forget, Mike, there's someone I want you to meet before you leave," Laurie called after them, raising her voice to be heard over the loud music.

Mike threw an annoyed look back at her, his fake scar twitching in irritation, then turned pointedly away.

"That was subtle," Catherine murmured, accepting a glass of wine from him. Red wine, of course, she noted in wry amusement. "Your sister wanted to fix you up with someone tonight?"

He sighed and glanced back at Laurie and Charlie, who had their heads together while Drew stood awkwardly nearby. "Don't let them get to you. They really are great, but they get pretty weird about the women I see. You know how families can be sometimes."

"Well, not exactly. Remember, mine is just me and my parents. And they tend to stay out of my personal life."

"I wouldn't trade my sisters for anything, of course, but they can be pains at times. But anyway, Laurie's just grumpy tonight because her boyfriend had to work and couldn't come to her big party. He's a meteorologist. Cole Peoples from channel seven?"

"I've seen him. He seems nice."

"Yeah, he's okay. Kind of obsessed with weather systems, but I suppose that comes with his job."

"There have been a few people who have accused me of being the same way about science."

"Mmm." He took a sip of his wine, his expression suddenly rather somber. "Oddly enough, I don't have a lot to say about maintenance work."

"As long as you enjoy what you're doing and you do it well, that's all that really matters, isn't it?"

"Yeah, well, this isn't the time to talk about work. Let's dance."

"Um, dance?"

He smiled, flashing those wicked teeth. "You know, moving in time to the music? Maybe a little body contact during the process?"

"I'm not a very good dancer. Especially to this type of music."

He took the plastic wineglass from her hand and set it aside. "Don't worry, Professor," he murmured, sliding his arm around her waist again. "No one will be grading you tonight."

Glancing back at his sisters, she wasn't so sure he was right about that.

Catherine learned during the dance—fortunately, a slower-tempo number—that while Laurie was the official hostess because she had provided the venue, Mike and Charlie had contributed to the expenses for the party. They had each invited some of their own friends to attend.

Mike seemed to know most of his sisters' friends, but he looked pleased to spot a group standing in a back corner of the room, beneath a cluster of black and orange balloons. "Hey, I see Bob and Brandon back there in that bunch. Come meet them. You'll like them."

She couldn't help remembering that he had made the same prediction about his sisters.

There was something inherently bizarre in meeting people for the first time while wearing costumes, Catherine thought, as Mike introduced her to a pirate and a marauder. "Catherine, these are my two best friends, Brandon Williams and Bob Sharp. Guys, Catherine Travis."

Pleased that he'd left off the title this time, she smiled. "It's nice to meet you both."

Brandon, a black-haired pirate with a stuffed parrot attached to his right shoulder, smiled at her and lifted a black patch to study her with both of his eyes. "A pleasure to meet you, too, Catherine."

Bob Sharp was squarely built and florid-faced. Messy near-orange hair spilled from beneath a horned metal hat to almost brush his shoulders. His costume was amusing—a ragged shirt, thick, furry vest, fake-leather kilt with a long plastic knife strapped to one side, leather sandals that laced up his hairy bare calves. He was leering at her in a way that should have made her uncomfortable, but somehow did not. Maybe because the mischievous twinkle in his eyes made her automatically inclined to smile back at him.

"So you're the one who's been helping Clancy study?" he asked.

She wasn't sure how much Mike had told his friends about her, so she nodded and said simply, "Yes."

"Then no wonder he's been so eager to hit the books. If I had a study partner like you, I might take a few classes myself."

His pirate friend snorted derisively. "You'd have to learn to read first."

"In your ear, Williams," Bob retorted, and grabbed Catherine's hand. "C'mon, honey. I've been wanting to dance with a beautiful vampire all evening. And since pretty-boy Clancy would probably turn me down, I'll choose you. I'll even let you take a bite out of my neck if you want."

"She'd have to disinfect it first," Mike muttered, giving Catherine a look of apology.

Wondering what she had gotten herself into, she allowed herself to be towed onto the crowded dance floor by Bob the Hun.

"So, Cathy," he said, wrapping both arms around her in a cross between a dance hold and a bear hug. "Mike told me you're a scientist. You must be really smart, huh?"

It was amazing how often people said that to her. Yet after all this time, she still hadn't really learned how to respond except to say, "I just like science. What do you do, Bobby?"

Grinning at her pointed nickname table turning, he replied, "I deliver snack foods to local retailers. Be nice to me and I'll hook you up with a case of those cream-filled chocolate cupcakes."

"Vampires don't eat cream-filled chocolate cupcakes," she responded, trying to match his silliness.

"Then be *real* nice to me and I'll scare you up some blood-filled ones."

She laughed. She liked Bob, even if he did seem a little…odd. At least he wasn't treating her as if she were planning something evil and dastardly for Mike, she thought with a glance across the room to where Laurie had already descended on him.

"Mike, this is my new friend Erin," Laurie said brightly, drawing forward a blushing blonde in a Dallas Cowboys cheerleader costume. "The one I told you about."

Mike managed to politely acknowledge the introduction while giving his sister a chiding look at the same time. Laurie was actually still trying to fix him up, even though he was here with Catherine? "Good to meet you, Erin."

"You, too, Mike." Despite the impressive cleavage revealed by her costume, she looked younger than twenty-four. She gazed up at him through heavily darkened eyelashes and gave him a smile that was probably intended to look sweetly shy—but didn't quite. "Laurie's been telling me all about you."

"Has she?" He wondered if his sister had mentioned that he'd been seeing someone.

Erin nodded. "She said you're into hiking and kayaking. I spent a week last summer kayaking and camping out with friends in Vancouver."

"Really? That must have been great."

"It was awesome. I took a lot of pictures. Maybe you'd like to see them sometime?"

"Um, have you met my friend Brandon?" He tugged his very willing friend closer and made the introductions.

Laurie glared at him, though her voice was still almost chirpy when she said, "I thought you could tell Erin about the best places to kayak around here, Mike. Didn't you say this is the best time of year to go?"

He was saved from having to answer when Bob returned from the dance floor with Catherine. He reached out quickly to draw her to his side. "Looks like you survived your dance with this crazy man."

Catherine's smile was only a bit strained as she glanced from Laurie to Erin and back to

Mike. "Bob offered to give me a case of blood-filled cupcakes."

Looping an arm around her shoulders, Mike scowled darkly at Bob. "Trying to bribe her away from me, Sharp?"

His friend grinned unrepentantly, apparently enjoying the undercurrents of tension. "If I thought that would work, I'd offer her a whole truckload of goodies."

Mike watched as Erin appraised the situation and then turned to Brandon with a bright smile. "Tell me, Brandon, do *you* like kayaking?"

Giving Mike a nod of gratitude, Brandon escorted the bubbly cheerleader onto the dance floor, much to Mike's relief and Laurie's dissatisfaction.

Chapter Nine

Catherine had no intention of being alone with Laurie that evening, but fate apparently had other plans. They ended up in the ladies' room at the same time, both poised in front of the mirror with tubes of lipstick in their hands.

Feeling the need to say something gracious, Catherine capped her lipstick. "Your party is very nice, Laurie. Everyone seems to be having a good time."

"Thank you." Tucking her tube of glittery gloss into her belt, Laurie turned to face her. "Nice costume. You and Mike obviously coordinated your outfits. His idea?"

"Actually, no. It's just coincidence that we both ended up in black and purple."

"Great minds, hmm?"

"I suppose so."

"My little brother seems to be quite taken with you."

Little brother. Definitely a message embedded there. Because Catherine couldn't think of anything to say in response, she let it go. "I'd better get back out. He's waiting for another dance."

"You know, as many women as Mike has dated, I'm not sure he's ever gone out with a scientist before."

Another message, not so subtle this time. Catherine felt her rare temper starting to simmer. Laurie's little barbs were starting to annoy her. *As many women as Mike has dated...* Indeed.

Because she simply didn't have the patience for catty games, she placed her hands on her hips and faced Mike's sister squarely. "Is there something you want to say to me, Laurie?"

Laurie looked surprised only for a moment,

then she lifted her chin. "I just can't help wondering why you've been spending so much time with Mike. I'd hate to think you were just stringing him along or anything."

"Well, isn't it obvious?" Catherine asked curtly. "I'm just using him as a pretty boy toy. After all, what else could I possibly see in him?"

Laurie's cheeks darkened—whether from embarrassment or anger, Catherine couldn't say. Maybe a combination of both. "Well, you are a Harvard trained scientist. Mike's a maintenance man who doesn't even have an undergraduate degree. You can't blame me for being concerned."

"Actually, I can. Not only are you selling Mike short, you're making some fairly unpleasant insinuations about me. I think your 'little brother' is capable of handling his social life without your interference—and I know for a fact that I am. Now, if you'll excuse me—"

She turned and shoved against the bathroom door, almost flattening an incoming Raggedy Ann in the process. Murmuring an apology, she moved across the room toward Mike.

* * *

Charlie had practically pounced on Mike the minute Catherine left for a few minutes to step into the restroom. Drew hovered nearby, looking ruefully at Mike, as if he had tried but failed to stop Charlie from meddling.

"Are you having a good time?" Charlie asked brightly to begin the conversation.

"Yeah, great party." Mike held up a frosted cookie shaped like a ghost. "Good cookies. Where'd y'all get them?"

"The bakery on Chenal. So, do you think Catherine's having fun?"

Munching the ghost's head, Mike nodded. He had taken out the fake teeth, the better to sample the food, and this was his second cookie from the snack trays arranged on the bar. "She seems to be," he said after swallowing.

"It's sort of hard to tell with her, isn't it?" Charlie spoke a little too casually. "I don't know if it's her costume or if she's just naturally reserved, but she doesn't seem to show her emotions much."

"She's a little reserved, but she's not that hard to read. She doesn't play games. She's very honest about what she's thinking."

Charlie brushed a bit of lint from the short green belted tunic she wore with green tights and low boots. "You've obviously fallen pretty hard for her in a short time. You aren't getting serious about her, are you?"

"Charlie," Drew muttered, his voice sounding strained.

She ignored him. "I just want you to be careful, Mike. I mean, you've never really been serious about anyone before, and I wouldn't want you to be hurt if it turns out she doesn't feel the same way."

"What your sister is saying," Bob said, joining them just in time to overhear, "is that there's a possibility the beautiful, brilliant doctor is just temporarily slumming with the young mainte-nance man for good times and hot sex. What Charlie hasn't made clear is why any of that would be a bad thing."

Drew snorted. Charlie scowled. Bob looked

inordinately pleased with himself. Mike wondered what had made him think that bringing Catherine to a party with his sisters would be a good idea.

The first thing he noticed when Catherine rejoined him was the glint of temper in her brown eyes—an expression he had already learned to recognize. Seeing Laurie tagging a few feet behind gave him a pretty strong clue of who had lit Catherine's fuse.

What was with his sisters tonight? They were usually such friendly, congenial women. Even with his previous girlfriends they hadn't liked— and there had been several—they had at least been civil.

Were they intimidated by Catherine's career? If so, that was just stupid. His sisters were all successful on their own. Gretchen was a loan officer, Amy was an R.N. in a neonatal unit, Charlie was a veterinarian's assistant and Laurie had just started selling real estate, and was doing quite well with it. All perfectly re-spectable professions.

But he couldn't imagine what else could be the problem. How could anyone not like Catherine? Couldn't they see how great she was?

He wasn't falling for her, he assured himself, a little uncomfortable with Charlie's accusation. He just really admired her. Liked her. Enjoyed being with her. That was pretty much all there was to it, he thought, then wished he felt a bit more confident about his muddled feelings.

Catherine looked at Charlie, who was still standing rather close to Mike, and gave her a glittering smile. "Is there anything *you* would like to say to me? Any more questions you feel compelled to ask?"

"Um," Charlie blinked. "No, I can't think of anything."

Nodding in satisfaction, Catherine turned to Mike. "I believe you've been waiting for a dance?"

He was mildly surprised, but he wasted no time taking her up on the offer. "As a matter of fact, I have been. Let's go boogie."

* * *

Catherine was more than ready to leave the party after a couple more dances with Mike, but she allowed Bob Sharp to wheedle her into one last dance with him first.

"Don't let them get to you, sugar," he advised kindly. "Mike's sisters are really decent. He's just let them get away with bossing him around for too long."

"Bossing him around? According to Mike, they spoiled him rotten. Indulged his every whim."

"Oh, they did," Bob agreed. "And in return, he let them fuss over him and fret about him, and tell him exactly how they thought he ought to live. Now, he didn't always take their advice, you understand. He just smiled and let them think he was paying attention to everything they said. But he's set his heels this time. He isn't going to let them try to push you around."

"He doesn't have to worry about that."

Grin flashing, Bob patted her back in a conspiratorial manner. "I don't doubt you can stand up for yourself. Bet you didn't let your sisters push you around."

"Actually, I was an only child. Maybe that's why I'm so perplexed by Mike's sisters."

Bob sighed heavily. "I'm real sorry to hear that."

"That I'm an only child? Why?"

"I was kind of hoping you have a hot single sister. I mean, I would make a play for you, but then Mike would feel the need to bust my head, so I guess that's out. You wouldn't have a girlfriend who likes her men a little on the crazy side, would you?"

Catherine smiled. "I only have two close friends. One is married, and the other…"

"What about the other one?" he prodded with eager curiosity. "Is she a lesbian or something?"

"No," Catherine said, unable to resist a laugh. "She's an attorney."

"A lawyer, huh?" He gave it a moment's thought, then shrugged. "Oh, hey, no one's perfect. Set it up."

"Set what up?" she asked in bewilderment.

"Double date. You and Mike, me and the

lawyer. We'd make it a triple with Brandon, but I doubt your other friend's husband would approve. He can just keep trying his luck with the wannabe cheerleader over there."

The thought of Julia on a date with Bob made Catherine's head spin. Talk about a match *not* made in heaven—or anywhere short of Bizarro universe... "I don't think so."

"I promise I'll wear pants," Bob vowed with an earnestness that amused her again. "You can ask her if she's interested, right? It might be fun."

"I'm sure any evening with you would be fun," Catherine answered honestly. "But I don't know if Julia would be interested in a blind double date. And to be honest, I don't even know if I'll be seeing Mike again after tonight."

"If it's up to him, you will be. So that means you must be the one having doubts. You're not letting the girls scare you off, are you?'"

She cleared her throat. "Um, Bob?"

He led her into a sweeping dance turn. "Yeah, sugar?"

"Butt out, okay?"

He accepted the order as good-humoredly as she had expected. "Yes, ma'am. But if you *do* see Mike again—and if your friend Julia is interested—give me a call, okay?"

She laughed softly, admiring his persistence. "Okay."

"And, Doc?" he added as the music ended.

"Yes?"

"If you and Mike do call it quits—you can still give me a call. I'd be willing to risk a busted head."

"You're a very nice man, Bob Sharp." And very good for her ego, which had taken a few blows that evening, she added silently.

He beamed. "I like you, too, Doc."

They were still smiling at each other when Mike joined them. Frowning from Bob to Catherine, he commented, "You two seem to be getting along."

"I've been wowing her with my deadly charm and animal magnetism." Bob patted Catherine's arm.

Mike made a derisive sound and turned to Catherine, pointedly dismissing his friend.

"The party's starting to wind down. Are you ready to go?"

"As a matter of fact, I am."

Catherine deliberately kept the conversation focused on Bob and Brandon during the short drive back to her apartment. Talking about Mike's friends seemed an innocuous enough topic. She really didn't want to get into a discussion about his sisters' behavior while he was behind the wheel.

Mike seemed to concur. He told her several amusing stories about his buddies, especially Bob, that made her smile despite the tension lingering inside her.

It was late now, and the trick-or-treaters had all gone home to sort their goodies. There weren't many people moving around in the apartment complex, and Catherine didn't see anyone she knew when Mike walked her from his truck to her door.

Her feet hurt. She wasn't used to wearing high heels for that long. Her face itched from the unusually heavy makeup, and she was ready to wash the gel out of her hair and put on a baggy T-shirt and dorm pants. She'd had enough dress up and make-believe for one day.

She put her key in her door lock. "Mike, I—"

"Do you mind if I come in? Just to talk for a few minutes?"

Okay, so much for a cowardly retreat. She nodded and opened her door.

Norman ran up to greet them, sniffing their clothes as if vicariously experiencing their evening through scent. Catherine greeted her pet briefly, then turned to Mike. "There was something you wanted to talk about?"

"Yeah." He unsnapped the cape at his throat and tossed it over an arm of her couch. His face looked grim, the false scar adding to his somber appearance. "I want to apologize for the way Laurie and Charlie acted. I swear, Catherine, I don't know what got into them, but I'm going to have a long talk with them both. They don't usually act like that."

"Don't yell at them. They were just being

honest about their doubts about us. I much prefer honesty to having people smile to my face, then trash me behind my back."

"They judged you before they even met you, and that wasn't fair."

"From what I understand, they were just acting like typical older sisters."

"Maybe. But I promise, next time they'll be on their very best behavior."

Catherine reached up to pull the black silk rose from her gelled hair.

Mike frowned, reading her silence a bit too easily. "There will be a next time, right? I was thinking maybe we could catch a movie Saturday night. Maybe go out to dinner first."

"I don't know if that's a good idea, Mike."

Though she was carefully avoiding looking at his face, she sensed his scowl. "Is this because of the way Charlie and Laurie acted tonight? What did Laurie say to you in the restroom?"

"It wasn't anything she said. It's just…well, I wouldn't want to come between you and your sisters. I know you're all very close."

"That isn't going to change just because you and I are seeing each other," he argued, looking stubborn.

"That's the point. I don't know if we are seeing each other."

"Damn it, this is about my sisters, isn't it? You let them get to you. Or Bob—was it something Bob said? I know he's kind of…well, nuts, but he's really a great guy once you…"

She shook her head. "Mike, I like Bob."

He looked taken aback. "You like *Bob?*"

"No, I don't mean I *like* Bob. I just—" Hearing her own words, she stopped and shook her head again. "I am not going to get into another Abbott and Costello routine with you. This argument is ridiculous."

He didn't smile, though she could tell he found her comment vaguely amusing. "What's really bothering you, Catherine? Is it me? I mean, I'll understand if you just aren't inter-ested in pursuing this any further. After all, you're a scientist and I—"

"Don't even finish that sentence." She planted

her fists on her hips and glared at him. "I've listened to your sisters put you down all evening. I'm not going to stand here and let you start doing the same thing."

"My sisters weren't putting me down," he said defensively. "They were just…"

"Just wondering out loud what the scientist could possibly see in the maintenance man?" It made her indignant all over again just thinking about it. "As if it's so hard to believe I could be attracted to your mind and your personality and…"

She never even realized what he was about to do until she found herself suddenly in his arms. "You were really starting to worry me," he said, and covered her mouth with his.

Surprise kept her immobile for a few moments. She wasn't sure what, exactly, she had said to initiate this—but she wasn't exactly complaining, either, she decided as her hands rose to his shoulders.

When he spoke again, it was against her lips, as if he were reluctant to break the contact between them even long enough to say, "I thought you were about to tell me you didn't want to see me again."

As he pressed his mouth against hers again, she thought dazedly that she actually had been trying to say something like that. Not that she didn't want to see him again, but that she wasn't sure it was a good idea to let this go any further.

There were probably half a dozen reasons why they shouldn't get involved. As for what they *did* have in their favor—well, she wasn't sure intense physical attraction was enough to sustain a relationship for very long, but it was certainly a heady experience for now.

His hands slid down her back, and she shivered. So maybe the two dates they'd had so far hadn't been unqualified successes. Maybe next time would be better.

Next time. As Mike slowly raised his head to give them both a chance to breathe, she realized that sometime during that kiss she had decided there would be a next time.

These things really shouldn't be determined on a physical basis, she chided herself. But with his arms still around her, his breath still warm on her face, his reactions to the embrace as obvious to her as her own, she thought maybe it was a good enough reason for now.

Mike settled his hands at her hips and pulled her a little more snugly against him—just in case she hadn't been aware of his condition, perhaps. "I could stay awhile longer," he suggested, seemingly trying to be tactful, though hardly subtle.

She was tempted. *Very* tempted. And she made no effort to hide it from him, any more than he was trying to conceal his desire for her. He gave her time to consider her response without pressure from him. After several long moments, she let out a slow, deep breath and said, not without regret, "I think you'd better go."

His expression resigned, he lifted a hand to run a fingertip down her jawline. "Too soon, huh?"

She swallowed and wondered if she would ever get used to the feel of his touch against her skin. "I think so."

Things were already getting complicated between them. She didn't think it would be at all wise to add new layers of complexity just yet. Maybe if she had been the type to enjoy a night of pleasure without letting her emotions get too deeply involved—but she wasn't. Her mind, body and heart were all intricately connected, and she wasn't ready to commit any one of those sides of herself to Mike after only two tentative dates.

Maybe he already knew her well enough to understand her thinking—or maybe he simply took her at her word without trying to understand her logic. After giving himself just another moment to hold her, he dropped his arms and stepped slowly backward. "I won't say I'm not disappointed, but I understand. So about that dinner and movie Saturday night…"

She started to accept, and then she remembered, "Oh, wait. I can't Saturday. My friend Karen is having a dinner party that evening."

"Oh. Well, maybe we can…"

"You could go with me to Karen's party," she blurted without giving herself time to think about it.

He hesitated. "Your friend wouldn't mind if you brought me along?"

"No. She told me I could bring a guest." Actually, Karen had strongly hinted that Catherine should bring Bill James, but that wasn't exactly relevant at the moment. "I've met some of your friends. Maybe you would like to meet some of mine."

"Yeah. Okay." She wouldn't exactly call his tone wildly enthusiastic, but he seemed agreeable enough to the plan. "What time?"

"She lives in Benton, so we should leave by six-fifteen at the latest. That should allow us time to avoid the worst of rush hour traffic. I'll drive this time since I know how to get there."

He nodded, letting her set the agenda without comment. "Okay. Um, is this a casual thing?"

She smiled then. "Well, you could wear your cape and pointed teeth, but you might look a little out of place. It's casual," she added when he gave her a look. "Definitely no jackets or ties."

Mike nodded again. "Okay."

"Then it's a date."

"It's a date." He brushed his mouth across hers one more time, then turned for the door and let himself out.

Catherine locked the door behind him, then wandered into her bedroom. She looked for a moment at the empty bed, aware of a wistfulness somewhere deep inside her—and then she turned firmly away. The image she saw in the full-length mirror startled her for a moment, even though she had been seeing herself like this all evening.

It was definitely time for her to scrub off her makeup and get out of this costume, she told herself. She wasn't thinking at all like herself tonight.

Mike was on the treadmill after midnight, his sneakered feet pounding the rubber as he ran, his measured breathing echoing in his ears. He was the only one making use of the exercise equipment at this hour. He was going to be tired tomorrow, but he'd been too wired to sleep.

He had been like this ever since he'd left

Catherine's apartment. Their kisses, the feel of her slender body in his arms, had left him almost quivering with adrenaline and testosterone. Hence, the treadmill.

Three miles into his run, he wondered if Catherine was worth the effort of pursuing her. They really didn't have much in common. Except for Bob—who liked everyone, especially women—his family and friends were convinced she was all wrong for him. She didn't like the kind of movies and activities he liked, not even the same kind of food. She liked sushi, for crying out loud.

Physically they connected. Sparks flew whenever they kissed. Hell, even a touch could make his pulse race. He hadn't been this attracted to anyone in a long time. And yet, here he was, burning off sexual energy on a treadmill in the middle of the night.

By the fourth mile, he had almost convinced himself to give it up. He didn't need this frustration in his life. Up until a few months ago, he had been perfectly content with everything just the way it was. He hadn't worried about classes or homework or studying or trying to impress anyone. He hadn't felt the need to apologize for his education or his career. He had thought of himself as a young man with his whole life ahead of him, plenty of time to accomplish whatever he eventually decided to do.

He never should have attended that stupid high school reunion. Nothing had been the same since.

Finally growing tired, he slowed to a walk to cool down. So now he had a whole list of reasons why he shouldn't continue to attempt a relationship of any kind with Catherine. But he couldn't stop thinking about the way he had felt when he'd been so certain she was going to tell him she didn't want to see him again socially.

It had made him feel sick. A little panicky. And when she had admitted that she was attracted to him despite their differences, he had been flooded with so much pleasure and relief that it made him uncomfortable just thinking about it now.

Don't get hooked, Clancy, he warned himself. *Not on this one.*

He had gone twenty-eight years without having his heart broken. He didn't want to change that now.

Chapter Ten

To give him credit, Mike was only five minutes late arriving at Catherine's apartment Saturday evening. Because she had come to know him well enough by now to have built in an extra fifteen minutes to their travel time, she didn't mind so much.

He'd had his hair trimmed, she noted immediately. It was combed so neatly he looked like a kid who had been spiffed up for a school picture.

He wore a brown sweater with a thin black stripe across the front with khaki slacks and brown moc-style shoes. While he was dressed casually enough for the occasion, she could tell he had given some thought to his clothes. Maybe even purchased something new to wear. She was touched by the care he had taken to make a good impression with her friends.

"You look very nice," she told him.

He smiled and brushed his mouth lightly across hers. "Thanks. So do you."

She had worn one of her new outfits—a long tiered skirt patterned in brown, orange and gold with an orange gauze shirt and a brown corduroy jacket that fit snugly and ended at her waist. Paired with her new brown boots, it was an outfit that worked well with Mike's—casual, but still nice. This was much more "her" than the vampy costume she had worn for Halloween, but still a bit more festive than her usual work clothes.

Mike settled comfortably into the passenger's seat of her small car, apparently content with being driven rather than being behind the wheel. She gave him free rein with the radio, and he tuned in the same rock station he had played in his truck. "I like this song," he said when a new number began.

"Who sings it?"

He seemed a little surprised that she didn't know. "It's Green Day. 'Wake Me Up When September Ends.' It's been around for a while."

"I don't follow music very closely. The last CD I bought was a compilation of Celtic music."

"Yeah? I like Celtic music. There are several really good Celtic groups who play in some of the local clubs."

Finally something they agreed on. She even liked the song playing on the radio. They both liked Celtic music and this one song by some group called Green Day. They were obviously a match made in heaven, she thought ironically.

The Kuppermans had recently moved into a four-bedroom house in a neighborhood just outside of Benton, a little over twenty miles southwest of Catherine's apartment. Though they had no children as yet, they used two of the extra bedrooms for home offices, and the other for a guest room. They were considering starting a family now that they had established their careers. With Wayne having just turned thirty-five and Karen thirty-two, they were aware that time was becoming an issue.

Several cars were already parked in the driveway. Catherine parked at the curb by the mailbox.

"Is there a special occasion for this party?" Mike asked as they walked to the front door.

"Karen and Wayne just moved into this house at the end of September and they've been decorating ever since. Karen said it's finally ready for their first dinner party."

"And this is someone you know from work?"

"Yes. She and I met at a science conference when we were both second-year grad students. We stayed in contact, then she convinced me to interview here when I was looking for a position two years ago. She introduced me to her longtime friend Julia Montgomery and the three of us have spent a lot of time together since."

She rang the doorbell, then smiled encouragingly at Mike. "You'll like everyone here. They're all very nice."

"I forgot to ask what your friend's husband does for a living."

Catherine answered just as they heard noises from the other side of the door. "He's a professor of philosophy."

She thought she heard Mike groan, but then Karen was in the doorway, greeting them with a bright smile.

"Catherine!" Karen said as if they hadn't just seen each other at work the day before. "I'm so glad you could come. And you must be Mike."

He gave her one of his high-voltage smiles, making her blush like a teenager. "It's a pleasure to meet you, Karen. Catherine's been telling me all about you."

"Has she? She hasn't told me near enough about you."

"Then maybe you should just ask me what you want to know."

"Maybe I will." Still smiling, she led them through a spacious, stone-floored entryway to a den decorated with moss-green walls, bright white trim and overstuffed upholstered furni-

ture. Built-in bookshelves filled one wall, over-
flowing with books and stereo equipment. A
big-screen TV was installed over the white-
brick fireplace, but it was turned off. This was
obviously the room where Karen and Wayne
spent their relaxation time.

Five people mingled in the den. Karen turned
in the doorway to speak to Catherine. "You
know everyone, Catherine. Why don't you introduce your friend while I check on dinner?"

A short, pleasantly dumpy man with a shiny
balding head, friendly myopic eyes and the
smile of a saint approached them with his right
hand extended. "Wayne Kupperman," he said to
Mike. "Welcome to our home."

"Thank you. I'm Mike Clancy."

A more feminine version of Wayne—short,
plump and sweet-faced with thin mousy hair
pulled into a loose bun—approached them with
a tall, thin, shy-looking man in tow. "Catherine,
it's good to see you again."

"You, too, Bonnie. Mike, this is Wayne's
sister, Bonnie Diamond and her husband Chris.

And this is our friend Julia Montgomery," she added, nodding toward Julia, who was eyeing Mike warily. "Everyone, this is Mike Clancy."

Mike shook hands all around. Julia barely touched his fingertips before moving away from him. Catherine could tell that Mike was a bit startled by Julia's frostiness. He was more accustomed to women giggling and flirting when he turned on the charm, she reflected wryly. His charisma had certainly worked with Karen, and seemed to now be affecting Bonnie, who was almost fifteen years his senior.

"Let me get you both a drink," Wayne offered eagerly, moving to a small wheeled serving cart set against the back wall. "What would you like?"

Catherine glanced at the wineglass in Julia's hand. "I'll have what Julia's having."

"That's good for me, too," Mike seconded.

"How are things at work, Catherine?" Bonnie asked, sipping her own drink.

"Pretty well. How about you?"

"Busy as always. Trying to keep up with all the new regulations for over-the-counter cold and allergy medications, and all the new prescription drug plans."

"Bonnie's a pharmacist," Catherine explained to Mike when Bonnie turned to answer a question from Julia. "Chris is an orthodontist, and Julia's an attorney."

"I see." He took another deep sip of his wine.

Karen appeared in the doorway a short time later to call everyone in to dinner, and they filed into the dining room, which was decorated in a sunny, Tuscan-themed style. The discussion about drug laws that had begun in the den carried over through the first course of dinner.

Catherine wondered at one point why Mike was being so unnaturally quiet. She certainly didn't believe he was shy; she had watched him meet a few new people at Laurie's party, and he'd been completely at ease with them. She knew he had friends and family members in skilled, white-collar professions, so it couldn't be that he was feeling self-conscious about his job, could it?

Was he intimidated tonight because these were her friends and he was anxious to make a good impression? Or was he just bored with a quiet evening of dinner and conversation?

The conversation turned to the food, which was excellent since Karen took pride in her culinary skills, especially with Middle Eastern dishes. Karen and Wayne had experimented with a strict Kosher diet early in their marriage, she had once confided to Catherine, and while they no longer followed those restrictions, she had become quite a creative cook. Catherine noticed that Mike eyed some of the exotic dishes a bit warily, but he ate enough of everything to be polite.

Despite Mike's lack of significant contribution, conversation was lively around the table. Julia, Bonnie and Chris got into a heated debate about rising medical costs and how they were influenced by lawsuits. Karen and Catherine discussed a recently published scientific breakthrough that had drawn national attention to one of their research colleagues. Wayne told an amusing story about an absent-minded professor in the Philosophy Department who had recently lectured an entire class period before realizing he was wearing a pajama top beneath his tweed blazer.

"I heard about that," Mike said, looking up from his plate. "One of the guys in my history class has that professor, and he's been entertaining us with weekly stories about the latest crazy thing Dr. Summers did."

Wayne smiled wryly. "Charles could have been used as the model for all those absent-minded professor stereotypes in Hollywood. He just doesn't seem to live in the same world as the rest of us."

"Shouldn't someone be concerned about his behavior?" Julia asked with a frown. "Maybe he should be evaluated for dementia or some other medical condition."

"Charles doesn't have dementia," Wayne said with another indulgent smile. "He isn't even quite fifty yet. And while I know there are rare cases of early-onset Alzheimer's, that's not an issue here. I've known Charles for almost fifteen years and he's been just like this the entire time.

A delightful man—brilliant and enthusiastic and good-hearted—but innately eccentric."

"I've met his wife," Karen volunteered. "The woman is a saint. She adores Charles, but she spends most of her life making sure he's fully dressed and in the right place at the right time. She raises their two teenagers and handles all the financial and practical business while Charles supports them all with his teaching and publications. He actually made the extended bestseller lists with one of his books a couple of years ago."

"In Search of a Hero; Mankind's Lifelong Quest for Role Models." Wayne beamed as he quoted the title. "A fascinating and insightful treatise, though I had a few minor points of disagreement with some of his generalizations, especially when it pertained to gender."

"Living with someone like that would drive me crazy," Julia pronounced with a disapproving shake of her head. "I'd have to strangle him, I'm afraid."

Knowing Julia, the others just smiled tolerantly. Catherine couldn't help wondering if Julia would ever be able to live with anyone. As fond as she was of Julia, she was aware that her friend tended to be too critical, especially when it came to men. Julia didn't just carry emotional baggage from past relationships; she hauled steamer trunks.

Mike's contribution to the conversation, minor as it had been, had drawn Wayne's attention to him now. "So you're taking classes at the university, Mike?"

Mike replied so easily that Catherine was probably the only one who noticed that the question made him self-conscious. "Yeah. I work as the maintenance supervisor at the apartment complex where Catherine and I live, which gives me some free time to take some late-afternoon and evening gen ed classes."

"What are you taking this semester?"

"American history and biology."

"Who do you have for history?"

"Dr. Levin."

Wayne nodded in approval. "She's very good. I've heard she's quite popular with the students."

"She makes the classes pretty interesting," Mike agreed. "And she seems to be genuinely interested in the students."

"As opposed to the professors who see students as simply an annoying infestation in their academic ivory towers?" Wayne asked wryly.

"Well, yeah. I've met a few like that."

"So have I, I'm afraid. Too many universities these days are so narrowly focused on revenues through sports and grants and corporations that they sometimes neglect the very students we were founded to serve. Students become nothing more than faceless, tuition-paying customers rather than integral partners in the dissemination of knowledge. We shuffle them though the system like products on a conveyor belt, and we lose entirely too many in the process because no one takes the time or care to find out what they need."

Karen smiled kindly at Mike. "He's on his soapbox now. This could go on for a while."

"Actually, I find it interesting." Mike addressed the comment equally to Karen and Wayne. "I dropped out of college the first time because no one seemed to care if I stayed after I lost my baseball scholarship."

"But wasn't it your responsibility to make sure you got an education?" Julia challenged him. "Most universities are too large to personally babysit every student."

"It was my responsibility, and I hurt no one but myself by dropping out," Mike agreed evenly. "Still, I might have understood better what I was giving up if anyone had taken the time to act like they cared."

"We're trying to do a better job of connecting with our students. Publicizing our student counseling services," Wayne said. "I've posted the hours and services provided there in my classroom and I mention it at the beginning of every semester and before every big exam. I've also tried to make myself available as much as possible to students who are struggling."

"Maybe you'll take one of Wayne's classes sometime, Mike."

"Maybe," Mike replied to Karen, though Catherine thought he looked doubtful that he would be registering for a philosophy class anytime soon.

"What's your major, Mike?" Chris asked, apparently trying to think of something to add to the conversation.

"I don't really have a major right now. I'm just getting some of the required stuff out of the way while I consider what I want to do next."

"Still trying to decide what you want to be when you grow up?" Julia spoke lightly, as if she were making a joke, but Catherine frowned at her, anyway.

Mike answered without looking at Julia. "Yeah, something like that."

Chris defused the momentary tension with a chuckle. "Join the club. Orthodontia was hardly my dream as a young man. I was thirty—about your age—before I finally settled down and went back to school. I've been practicing for fifteen years, but I've got another decade or so left in me before retirement."

"Actually, Mike's still a couple of years away

from thirty," Julia murmured. "At least, that's what Catherine said."

"You're only twenty-eight?" Chris looked a bit startled that Mike was even younger than he had guessed.

Mike nodded.

"Well then, you've got plenty of time to start a new career. If that's what you want to do, of course."

Shrugging, Mike said, "I certainly don't intend to do maintenance work for the rest of my life."

Catherine thought a change of subject was in order, for Mike's sake. "So, Wayne, how do you like your new car?"

"Oh, it's a honey," Wayne answered, instantly diverted. "It gets very good gas mileage, so I don't feel so bad about driving so far to work every day. And it's much quieter than my last car."

"That's because your last car was trying to shake itself into a million little pieces," Karen said dryly. "And us along with it. Is everyone ready for dessert? I made strawberry tarts, and I have fresh coffee for anyone who would like some."

Catherine pushed her chair back from the table. "Let me help you, Karen."

"I'll help, too," Julia said, jumping to her feet and reaching for dirty dishes.

Catherine had hoped Julia would make that offer.

Catherine waited only until they were in the kitchen and out of hearing of the dining room before rounding on Julia. "Get off his back, Julia. He's not one of the cocky jerks you dislike so much, so stop treating him like one."

Julia scowled. "I haven't been doing anything but making conversation with him."

"Asking him what he wants to be when he grows up? Please."

"Well, you would think he'd have an idea by now, wouldn't you? By his age, I'd already finished law school. You had a Ph.D. and a post-doctoral position behind you."

"And Mike has been working at perfectly re-spectable construction jobs since he left college the first time. He's very good at his maintenance job now. He takes pride in his work, and he tries to get to everything as quickly as possible. The on-site manager told me he's the most competent and responsible person she's ever hired for the position. He has no reason to be ashamed, and I wish you wouldn't treat him as if he should be."

Julia looked at her in concern. "You're not getting serious about this kid, are you, Catherine?"

Her cheeks warming, Catherine picked up a tray loaded with strawberry tarts. "He's a friend, and he deserves to be treated with the same respect as my other friends," she said curtly.

"You're absolutely right, Catherine." Karen handed Julia a tray of coffee cups while she picked up a steaming carafe. "He's a guest in my home, and I want him to be completely at ease here."

Going on the defensive, Julia followed them to the doorway. "I've hardly attacked him. Just asked a few questions to draw him into the conversation."

Catherine gave her a look that made it clear she didn't quite buy that innocent disclaimer.

Sitting in the passenger's seat of Catherine's car, Mike felt as though he had escaped a painfully awkward situation to blessed freedom. No one was looking at him curiously now, no one was asking him questions, no one was around to wonder what a guy like him was doing with Catherine.

Catherine had been driving with a somber expression that made him wonder what she was thinking. He didn't ask. He wasn't sure he wanted to know.

"Mike," she said, finally breaking the silence.

"Mmm?"

"I hope you weren't offended by the things Julia said tonight. She has become a good friend of mine, and I'm very fond of her, but I'm aware that she can be…difficult. She's very protective of her friends, and I think she has it in her head that you're just, I don't know, using me somehow."

"Because you make a decent salary and I'm doing maintenance work to pay rent and tuition? Does she think I'm some sort of freeloader?"

"Julia knows that no true gigolo is going to hit on a research scientist," Catherine said dryly. "We aren't exactly known for making tons of money. As an attorney, she's run into more men looking for a meal ticket than I have."

"Well, you can assure her that I'm not looking for anyone to support me," Mike said grumpily. "I've been paying my own way for almost ten years, and I plan to keep it that way. I might not have anything left over at the end of the month, but I don't take any hand-outs, either."

"Actually, I'm not going to tell Julia anything of the kind. It's none of her business—and as I said, she doesn't really think you're after my money, such as it is."

"So what is she worried about?"

"Julia has seen too many vulnerable women

hurt by men who found it amusing to toy with them for a while and then move on. She's had a couple of unhappy relationships, herself, and I'm afraid they've left her suspicious and a little bitter."

"And this is the woman you've thought of fixing up with Bob?" he asked in disbelief.

Catherine looked away from the road ahead long enough to give Mike a puzzled frown. "What are you talking about? I never said I wanted to fix her up with Bob."

"He said you have a lawyer friend you want him to meet. Were you talking about another lawyer friend?"

"No. *No*," she repeated more firmly. "Bob's either confused or he's deliberately misrepresenting the conversation I had with him. He asked if I had any single friends, and I said I had only one close single friend, an attorney, but that I didn't think they would hit it off."

Because Bob had a notorious habit of hearing only what he wanted to hear, Mike decided Catherine's version was the more likely one.

"Good call," he muttered. "I can't think of a more mismatched couple than Bob and Julia."

"Neither can I."

He wondered if Catherine was asking herself just then if they were as wrong for each other as Bob and Julia would have been. He doubted he was the only one with that question nagging at the back of his mind.

He was becoming discouraged with this whole situation. As strongly as he was drawn to Catherine, there just seemed to be too many counts against them. This was the third time they'd been out, and each time there had been some obvious indications that their lives didn't exactly mesh. She had hated the haunted house he thought would be so much fun. His sisters thought she was too reserved and intellectual for him. Her friends seemed to think she was either having an impulsive fling with the maintenance guy or being the victim of a manipulative, opportunistic gigolo.

They didn't say much as she parked the car and they climbed out on their opposite sides.

Catherine glanced up toward her apartment and he followed her example, spotting movement in the darkened living room window.

"Looks like Norman's waiting up for you."

She nodded. "He's acted kind of restless lately. Maybe the shorter days are unnerving him."

"A cat with seasonal affective disorder? Maybe he needs some serotonin-laced kibble?"

She laughed, and the sound pleased him, as it always did when he succeeded in drawing a laugh from her. "Maybe. I'll see if I can find a kitty shrink in the yellow pages."

Glancing up at the window again, he frowned. "Looks like your blind is hanging crooked. I hope Norman hasn't broken it again."

"He's probably just been bumping against it. I tied the cords up so he couldn't accidentally hurt himself with them."

"I'd better come up and check it out."

Catherine looked at him, and he sighed. "I'm not looking for an excuse to get into your apartment," he told her a bit testily. "If you'd rather check the blinds yourself, then call the office if there's a problem, that's fine."

"Don't be silly. I would appreciate you checking the blinds for me. I just didn't want you to feel obligated when you aren't on duty."

A little sheepishly he muttered an apology for his grumpiness and followed her up the steps.

Meowing loudly, Norman twined around their ankles when they walked in.

"He *is* kind of wound up, isn't he?" Mike knelt to stroke Norman's silky fur, scratching behind the ears and beneath the chin to elicit rumbling purrs of pleasure.

"You'd think he never had any attention," Catherine said with an exasperated shake of her head.

Straightening, Mike looked at the window blinds. The slats were a little crooked, probably because the cat had been pushing against them either out of boredom or to better see around them, but nothing was broken. He straightened the slats, retied the cords and turned back to Catherine. "Have you been having any other maintenance problems?"

"No. Everything is working satisfactorily."

"Good to hear." He pushed his hands into his pockets. He really hadn't used the blinds as an excuse to get in. Now that he was here, he wasn't sure what to do next.

"Can I get you anything?" Catherine asked, sounding almost as awkward as he felt. "Coffee? Herbal tea?"

"No, thanks. Your friend is a really good cook. She pretty well filled me up."

Catherine looked pleased. "Karen is a wonderful cook. She loves to experiment with unusual recipes. I wasn't sure you'd like the food."

"It was different, but everything was actually pretty good. Well...except for that sort of bluish stuff. No offense, but that was pretty nasty."

Catherine laughed again, her eyes crinkling ruefully at the corners. "I've got to agree with you on that one. What *was* that?"

"I was afraid to ask. But I noticed that no one ate much of it. Chris scraped his onto Bonnie's plate when no one else was looking."

"You're kidding. I didn't see that."

"Neither did Bonnie. She gave him a dirty look when she finally noticed. She hid it under a lettuce leaf."

"Karen knows not everything turns out as well as she hopes. She has a good sense of humor about it."

"She seemed nice. Her husband, too. Actually, everyone was decent—except maybe for Julia—even though I didn't have much in common with a group of professors and ortho-dontists and pharmacists."

"You're selling yourself short again. You just said they're nice people. Why would it matter what they do for a living?"

He hesitated, then sighed. "I guess I'm still smarting over my reunion. There was this girl— er, woman—from my class…"

"Did she say something derogatory to you?" Catherine asked quietly.

He wasn't at all sure he wanted to tell this story, but maybe it would help Catherine under-stand a little better why he'd been so sensitive about his career. Why he had been braced for condescension from her professional friends. "She and I had been flirting all day. Drinking a little too much. I had a thing for her in high school, but we'd never hooked up then. The reunion was an all-day thing, and we hung out for a couple of hours. Had a couple of dances that evening and things were looking promising—and then everyone started talking about their jobs. I really thought Marcia knew by then what I did, but I guess it had never come up.

"Someone said something about being a doctor, and Marcia said she was in pharmaceutical sales. That's when she turned to me and asked what I did. She said she knew I had gone to college to play baseball and she wondered if I'd turned pro."

"She thought you were still a ballplayer? Wouldn't that have been mentioned by that point?"

"Like I said, we hadn't been talking about careers. Up until then, it had all been remember-when stories and gossip about the ones who hadn't made it to the reunion. I guess she thought I looked the part of a ballplayer. It was a real casual affair and I'd worn a St. Louis Cardinals jersey-type shirt with jeans and athletic shoes. She figured I'd finished college, at the least, and had gone on to some white-collar career. When she found out I dropped out after one semester and had been working construction and maintenance jobs ever since—well, let's just say the flirting ended fast. She treated me like I had some sort of communicable disease for the rest of the evening."

"That was very shallow of her."

"She was always a little shallow. I just thought she'd outgrown it. I was wrong. I even saw her giggling with her old cheerleader friends later, and I figured she was telling them what a loser I'd turned out to be."

"Mike, you are *not*—"

He held up a hand to silence her automatic protest. "It wasn't so much the way Marcia acted that made me think about how I was wasting the best years of my life. It was looking at all the other guys who were doing the same thing. The ones who spend their time drinking and partying, drifting from one dead-end job to another just biding time till the weekend, not caring about the future. I mean, Bob and Brandon are great guys, you know? The best. But when I asked Bob if he'd started thinking about stuff like retirement or health plans or other things that might be headed our way, he just laughed and quoted that old saying about living fast, dying young and leaving a good-looking corpse."

"What did you say to that?"

Shrugging, Mike tried to smile. "I asked him where he was going to find a good-looking corpse to leave. It wouldn't do any good to try to have a serious conversation about stuff like that with him. He just turns everything into a joke."

"But you have fun with him."

"Oh, always. Bob's really a great guy. Wouldn't hurt a flea. Doesn't judge anyone, treats everybody the same. He just happens to be happy living in the present and letting the future take care of itself."

"We both have nice friends. They're just different, in some ways."

In a *lot* of ways, he thought. But their friends were no more different than he and Catherine, themselves.

He reached out to touch her hair, letting the silky brown strands ripple through his fingers. "It's so much easier when it's just the two of us, isn't it?"

She nodded slowly. "I suppose it is. We've never had any trouble talking when it's just us."

"That should mean something, shouldn't it? I mean, shouldn't it matter more that you and I get along than anything our friends have to say?"

"Not just friends," she reminded him, sounding wistful. "You can't just ignore your family."

"My sisters," he said dismissively. "They would come around. My parents would probably love you."

Even the mention of his parents made her go a little pale. Apparently, it had been too soon to even suggest that she meet them. Catherine was definitely the take-things-slowly type, while he was more of the jump-in-feet-first persuasion. No surprise there, of course.

"Maybe we should just leave everyone else out of this for a while," he suggested quickly to reassure her. "Maybe we could spend more time together, just the two of us, before we try mingling with our friends again. And Norman, of course," he added when the cat meowed as if in protest.

She rested a hand on his chest, somberly studying the way her fingers looked against his brown sweater. "We can't just ignore the rest of the world. We both have lives outside this apartment."

"Do we?" He slipped his other arm around her, drawing her closer. "When we're here, like this, I can't seem to think of anyone or anything but you. All those other people, those irritating complications—they just don't matter when I'm holding you like this."

He felt a slight tremor run through her hand. "That isn't a very sensible way of looking at things."

"I'm not feeling very sensible right now," he murmured, looking down at the top of her bent head.

She raised her face then, her darkened eyes meeting his. "What *are* you feeling right now?"

The answer popped into his head without the need for thought. "Hungry," he muttered. And he captured her mouth with his own.

Her hesitation lasted only a moment—but still long enough to almost stop his heart. It started again with a hard thump when she raised her arms around his neck and melted willingly into his embrace.

Chapter Eleven

All her life, Catherine had been practical, sensible, responsible. She rarely acted on impulse, never flirted with danger, never, ever allowed her emotions to overrule her common sense.

So, it was entirely out of character for her to take Mike by the hand and lead him into her bedroom, closing the door very firmly in her curious cat's face. She'd half expected Norman to throw a yowling fit, since he hated nothing more than a closed door in "his" apartment, but for once her pet was discreetly cooperative.

Mike hadn't said anything, but his gaze was

focused intently on her face when she turned to him. The room was in shadows, since she hadn't turned on the overhead light.

Her furniture almost filled the smallish bedroom—solid, mission-style pieces in light-stained wood, accented with hand-pieced quilts and primitive art. An iron lamp with a three-way bulb sat on the nightstand, turned on the lowest setting to provide a soft glow. Just enough to let her see that Mike's expression was torn between desire and concern.

"Are you sure about this?"

She slipped her hands beneath the hem of his sweater, letting her palms glide across the warm, smooth skin beneath. She felt his muscles tighten spasmodically in response to her touch, even as her own went liquid. "You aren't the only one who's hungry."

Mike groaned. "I've never been strong on either nobility or self-discipline. So if you aren't…"

She lifted her mouth to his, smothering his reservations in a kiss that let him know she was fully aware of what she was doing. She had made her choice, as uncharacteristic as it was. She wouldn't be changing her mind tonight.

His sweater fell to the floor, and Catherine caught her breath in response to what she had revealed. The sports and exercise that Mike enjoyed so much paid off in a firm, broad chest and a flat, taut stomach. The only flaw was a jagged, slightly raised four-inch scar that ran along the top of his rib cage. Yet, rather than detract from his appeal, the scar only added a new level of interest.

"Long story," he murmured, when she touched the scar curiously. "It involves a mountain bike, a patch of mud and a possum."

"I'd love to hear it," she said, and raised her mouth to his again. "Later."

His hands weren't quite steady when he helped her out of her jacket. She felt the tremors again when he fumbled at the fastening of her skirt. She liked that. She didn't want to think this was just another Saturday night for him.

It had been a long time since she'd been naked in front of anyone other than her doctor—and even then she was semimodestly covered with a paper gown. She stayed fairly slim, more from genetics than diet, but she didn't work out as religiously as Mike did. And while thirty certainly wasn't old, she didn't have the body of a teenager anymore, either.

She felt her face flame as Mike unfastened the first button of her shirt. "I'm a little nervous, I think," she confessed.

"*You're* nervous?" He gave her a crooked grin that made her heart clench. "I've never done anything like this with a professor before. I'm a little worried that I won't make the grade."

She smiled faintly, letting the blouse slide from her shoulders to leave her standing in nothing but a nude-colored bra and matching panties. "I doubt very much that you have anything to worry about on that count."

He pressed a kiss at the corner of her mouth, his hands making a leisurely cruise from her shoulders down her back to her hips. "Let's not either of us worry about anything tonight," he murmured against her lips. "Let's just enjoy."

Because that sounded like an excellent plan to her, she pushed any remaining reservations to the back of her mind and wrapped her arms around his neck. The move brought their bare bellies together, and the contact made her knees go weak. He still wore his slacks, and the fabric was crisp against her legs, making her impatient to get rid of them.

Whether because of her admission of nerves or because he was simply taking his own advice to savor this experience, Mike took his time. His hands rested very lightly on her hips as he concentrated on kissing her. Their mouths fused, probed, then separated only long enough to allow them to explore a new angle.

He didn't seem to be in any hurry to move on, but Catherine was rapidly losing patience. Maybe that was his intention—letting her gain enough confidence to assert herself. If that had been his plan, it was definitely working.

She slipped her hands between them and unfastened his belt. He helped her by kicking his slacks aside when she loosened them.

She was still trembling, but it was more from anticipation now than nerves. One gentle push from her was all it took to send him tumbling to the bed; probably because he didn't try at all to resist.

Their kisses turned hotter, deeper. Their hands moved more frantically. By the time their undergarments joined the other clothing on the carpet, Catherine had long since forgotten her earlier self-consciousness. As it happened, his hard, toned body fit very well against her softer one.

His skin was hot, warmed from the inside. She nestled more snugly against him, soaking up that delicious heat and letting it fuel her own.

No thinking tonight, she reminded herself. No analyzing or second-guessing. This had been building from the morning she had opened her door and found a drop-dead gorgeous man standing on the other side. She hadn't imagined then that he would be attracted to her in return, or that they would be drawn together despite the odds against them. But she didn't want to try to resist him any longer; not when this was something she wanted more than her next breath.

And speaking of breath…She was finding it very hard to catch her own as Mike nibbled his way from her earlobe to her shoulder to her collarbone and then lower. Her fingers tangled in his hair, and her legs wrapped themselves around his. If he found any imperfections in her body, he certainly didn't give any indication. The words he murmured were all appreciative, and so was his expression when he looked at her.

He had brought protection—whether as a matter of habit or because he had anticipated this, she didn't even want to know. No thinking, she reminded herself again. Better to just be grateful that he had been so well prepared.

He moved over her, bracing himself on his elbows, cupping her face between his hands. "Have I told you how pretty your eyes are?"

She smiled up at him. "They're just ordinary brown eyes."

"No. Not ordinary. They're beautiful. That first day I met you? After I left here, all I could think about for the rest of the day was you." He dropped a kiss at the corner of her right eye. "Your pretty eyes."

He brushed his lips across hers. "Your beautiful smile."

He moved against her, making her arch reflexively beneath him. "Your fantastic body. And that was before I got to know you, and found out how special you are," he added, resting his forehead against hers.

She placed her hands on his hips, her fingers digging lightly into his flesh. "Mike?"

"Mmm?"

Her voice was a bit strangled. "As much as I appreciate the compliments—could you stop talking now?"

His low laugh had a husky edge to it. "Yes, ma'am," he said, and then rendered them both speechless with a smooth thrust forward.

Catherine lay with her cheek on Mike's shoulder, almost idly reflecting on how dramatically one's life could change in just one evening. How much *she* had changed.

She would never think about lovemaking the same way, that was for certain. Before tonight, it had always been something she had considered usually pleasant, sometimes awkward, but not particularly important. Though her previous encounters had been few, she'd had no particularly traumatic sexual experiences. Nor had she had any particularly spectacular ones.

Until tonight. Making love with Mike could truly be considered spectacular. And maybe a little traumatic, as well, considering that she wasn't sure she would ever be satisfied with less from now on.

She wasn't ready to admit that she had fallen in love with him. After all, she'd known him for only a couple of months, and their time together hadn't exactly been idyllic. But she was aware that her feelings for him were more than mere attraction, more than simple friendship. She was teetering on the edge, and it wouldn't take much to push her over. A scary thought. Something told her the landing would be abrupt and ultimately painful.

She felt his lips on her forehead. "You're being awfully quiet. Are you okay?"

"I'm better than okay," she said, keeping her tone light. "I feel great, actually."

"Me, too." He snuggled her closer and rested his cheek on her hair. "I should probably go, but I've got to admit I don't really want to."

She should probably encourage him to leave, for several reasons. One of which was the gossip that could ensue if her neighbors realized that Mike had spent the night. And yet she heard herself saying, "I don't want you to go."

"I wouldn't want to make things awkward for you if anyone saw me here."

"We're not worrying about anyone outside this apartment tonight, remember? But I'm not particularly worried about what the neighbors say about me. I hardly know them, anyway." Who was she trying to convince—him or herself? Maybe she'd better not analyze that question too closely.

"I don't make a habit of this, you know," he said, sounding suddenly serious. "I haven't been with any of the other tenants of the complex. You're special to me, Catherine."

She was glad to hear that, even though she hadn't asked. She certainly didn't want to think of herself as just another notch on his tool belt. Julia probably wouldn't believe his assurance that Catherine was in any way special to him, but Catherine took him at his word. Julia would accuse her of being naive, of course, but—

She frowned in exasperation. What was she doing thinking about Julia? Hadn't she just said that they weren't supposed to worry about anyone else tonight?

His patience at being ignored having all run out, Norman began to meow on the other side of the door. "I'd better let him in or he'll keep that up all night."

Mike chuckled. "Since neither of us wants to risk his wrath, I suppose you'd better do what he demands."

The moment the bedroom door opened, Norman padded across the room and leaped onto the bed. Mike greeted him with a chuckle.

Leaving them to entertain each other, Catherine moved into the bathroom and closed the door. She was giving herself privacy for her bedtime preparations—and a few moments alone to make sure her composure was firmly under control. Searching her freshly scrubbed face, she was satisfied that she looked serene and almost nonchalant about having Mike in her bed. Which proved that she had more acting ability than she had ever suspected.

After donning a short nightgown, she crawled beneath the covers with Mike, who had returned from his own trip to the bathroom and was now lying on his back with Norman curled on his chest. Mike reached out and pulled Catherine onto his right shoulder, snuggling her close with his right arm while his left hand rested lightly on her contented pet.

Catherine closed her eyes and listened to Mike's heart beating steadily in his chest, the sound almost drowned out by Norman's loud purring. She realized that she was very close to purring herself. Yet just beneath the pleasant sounds she was aware of a small, insistent voice warning her that this wasn't wise. That she shouldn't allow herself to become too addicted to Mike's presence.

This couldn't last, that inner voice reminded her. She would be alone in her bed again soon enough—with the exception of Norman, of course—and if she wasn't careful, she was going to find herself hurting and lonely on those nights. Despite her longing for someone to share her life with, she had been fairly happy and satisfied before. Her heart had been intact, and she wanted it to stay that way.

Even as that thought crossed her mind, a hard ache deep inside her chest made her wonder if it was already too late to protect that vulnerable organ.

Mike stayed all night. They slept in, then locked Norman out of the room for a while again. By the time they were finally ready to leave the bed, it was late morning.

Mike left only long enough to change into fresh clothing in his own apartment, since Catherine had invited him to join her for lunch. He was gone less than an hour, and she used that time to call her lab and arrange for someone else to check on her ongoing experiment. She rarely took an entire day away from the lab, but she had quite a few favors to call in, since she was often asked to do things by the others who knew she could usually be counted on to be there.

By the time Mike returned, she had a good start on lunch. Becoming familiar with his culinary preferences, she kept the menu simple. Baked chicken breasts with wild rice and vegetables, and crusty wheat rolls. Using some prepackaged mixes for convenience, she had the meal ready in a short time.

"This is great, Catherine," he said, digging into the food with visible appreciation. "You didn't tell me you were such a good cook."

She laughed. "I'm not a gourmet chef, like Karen. Most of this meal came out of boxes or the freezer."

"Well, it's good," he insisted. "I tend to eat too many pizzas and sandwiches on my own."

Catherine stabbed her fork into a tender baby carrot. "No veggies? My mother would be appalled."

"So would mine." He chewed, swallowed, then took a sip of his iced tea before asking, "What's your mother like? Pretty much all I know about her is that she doesn't approve of trick-or-treating."

"I don't know. How do you describe your mother? She's smart. Funny, in a quiet way. Loving, yet very firm with her rules and expectations. Her students like her, but they know she won't let them get away with much. I was the same way."

"Strict, huh?"

"Not excessively so. More so than many parents, I suppose."

"My mom's pretty firm about her rules, too. I knew if I ever got into trouble at school, I could expect to double that at home. She didn't tolerate cursing, drugs or drinking from her kids, and we'd better be home by curfew or suffer the consequences."

Amused, she asked, "What were the consequences?"

"A 'mama lecture.' They could go on for hours, and leave our ears ringing. For a little bitty woman, she could get pretty darned loud."

She could tell by his tone that he was crazy about his mother, something she had already figured out about him. "What about your father?"

"Mom's total opposite. He'd have let us get away with just about anything, so it's a good thing she was so strict or we'd have all been hellions. Especially the girls. They all have Dad wrapped around their little fingers. The only time he got strict with them was when they started dating, and he had a way of making their dates shake in their sneakers with his suspicious looks and his pointed questions."

"My father is so much like my mother that it's almost scary," Catherine confided. "They finish each other's sentences. They like the same books and movies and music. They never quarrel."

"Never?" He looked startled by that.

"Never. At least, not about anything important. They do enjoy debating current events. They take turns arguing the liberal and conservative interpretations."

"Damn, Catherine, that's scary."

She laughed. "Tell me about it. My friends thought I had the weirdest parents ever. Especially when Dad cracked jokes about the Pythagorean theorem and Euclidean geometry. You would be surprised at the corny and obscure puns he can make with math terms."

"What do you suppose they would think about you seeing me? I mean, I bet they expect you to hook up with another scientist or a doctor or a professor."

"Don't start that again."

"I'm just asking what they would think."

She gave the question serious consideration before replying. How *would* her parents react if they learned that she was sleeping with a twenty-eight-year-old college freshman maintenance worker?

"Mother would probably warn me not to let myself be too distracted from my work," she said after a moment. "Dad would respect your decision to return to school, and he would try to talk you into declaring a math major. I think they would both like you, and both be rather surprised that we have enough in common to want to spend time together."

Mike grimaced. "I *did* ask," he muttered. "And you always give an honest answer, don't you?"

"I assume you wouldn't ask if you didn't want an honest reply."

His smile was a little crooked, but he seemed more bemused than perturbed by her innate frankness. "Something tells me you're very much like your parents in a lot of ways."

"I'm afraid so," she said, looking down at her plate.

Mike reached out to cover her hand with his own. "I wasn't saying that's a bad thing. Your folks sound like very interesting people."

She thought suddenly of their agreement the night before to ignore the outside world and concentrate on each other. She decided she would like to continue that policy for a little longer. She changed the subject rather abruptly. "Have you thought yet about what classes you're going to take next semester? Or whether you are going to take any more?"

He drew his hand back to his side. "Yeah, I'm going to take a few hours. I haven't really decided what yet, but I've got to make a decision pretty soon. Any recommendations?"

"I suppose you'll want to take more general education classes that are required for an eventual degree."

He nodded. "I'm sure it would be easier to choose classes if I'd declare a major."

"You have plenty of time for that."

"Do I?" Though he spoke lightly, his expression was somber. "I'm not getting any younger, you know."

"There's a graduate student in our doctoral program who's just turned fifty. She didn't receive her undergraduate degree until she was forty-five, after raising two children and working as a lab technician for almost twenty years. This was something she always wanted to do, and now she's making that dream come true."

"Good for her. How much longer does she have?"

"If all goes well, she should graduate in the spring."

"At least she had a good reason to take so long. Raising her kids, I mean. And she knew what she wanted to do."

"Surely you've thought about why you're taking classes. Do you plan to earn a degree?"

He nodded and pushed his empty dessert plate away. "I'd like to. I mean, I know I signed up for this semester on an impulse because I was still steamed about the reunion. But now that I'm back in school and doing pretty well, I'd like to make it count, you know?"

"I see no reason why you shouldn't earn a degree if you want."

"It's going to take forever if I only take two classes a semester. I suppose I should look into student loans so I can take more hours and cut back to part-time maintenance work. That way I could have a degree in four years—maybe a little sooner if I go summers."

"That sounds like a workable solution. Do you have some idea of the direction you want your studies to take? A liberal arts degree? Or something more specific, aimed toward a certain career?"

He hesitated for a long moment, then shrugged. "I haven't really thought about it."

She nodded and reached for their empty plates. If Mike didn't want to talk about his future plans, she certainly wasn't going to push him. "Would you like coffee or anything?"

"No, thanks. I'm so full now I couldn't even hold coffee." He helped her carry the dishes to the dishwasher. When the kitchen was spotless again, he reached out to wrap his arms loosely around her. "Getting tired of me yet?"

Resting her hands on his chest, she smiled up at him. "Hardly."

"Want to hang out?"

"Hang out?" she repeated, raising her eyebrows.

"Yeah. We could watch some TV or go catch a movie or play cards—whatever you like to do on a lazy Sunday afternoon."

She tilted her head thoughtfully. "I don't have many lazy afternoons. I usually go into the lab for a few hours every day—or I catch up on laundry or housework or paperwork."

"All work and no play?" He clucked his tongue in disapproval. "You know what they say about that."

"Are you implying that I'm dull?"

He laughed and drew her closer. "No. That is one thing I would never call you."

And that, she thought, was one of the things that drew her to Mike. He didn't find her dull.

Chapter Twelve

It was surprisingly easy to ignore the outside world when they really made an effort, Catherine discovered that afternoon. It was also relatively simple to find activities both she and Mike enjoyed, especially for a few hours.

They both liked games. Catherine owned several. She and her friends occasionally got together for a stress-relieving evening of games and desserts, she told him.

"But I warn you," she added as they set up the Monopoly board. "We tend to get very competitive."

"Honey, you haven't seen competitive until you've played the Clanster."

"'The Clanster?'" she repeated, thinking she must have heard him wrong—and trying to ignore the illogical little thrill of having him call her honey.

He chuckled. "Bob," he said, as if no further explanation was needed. And of course, it wasn't.

They played Monopoly. Mike won. They played Yahtzee. Catherine stomped him.

Afterward, they went out for ice cream. After all, who didn't like ice cream, even in November?

Mike ordered double chocolate fudge chocolate chip. Catherine requested strawberry. They took their time enjoying the treats, their heads close together at the tiny ice cream parlor table. It was easier to ignore everyone else that way—not that either of them knew anyone else there.

It took them a bit longer to agree on a film to see after the ice cream stop. Catherine loved quirky, arty films; Mike preferred gritty action. They compromised on a family-oriented, big-budget adventure film that turned out to be a pleasant diversion for a couple of hours.

They couldn't really analyze the plot afterward, as Catherine usually liked to do with her friends. In this case, there hadn't been much plot to analyze. As for the dialogue—well, she supposed some things shouldn't be critiqued too seriously on this sort of film. But the special effects had been awesome, and she had to admit that the lead actor had been handsome enough to make the two hours pass quite nicely.

"That wasn't bad, actually," Mike conceded. "Though I could have done without that kid kicking the back of my seat through the first half."

"Or the cell phones that kept ringing with those annoying little ditties. Why can't people remember to turn theirs off before the film begins?"

"That's why my mother refuses to go to a movie theater these days. Noisy food chewing and cell phones ringing and babies crying and people talking through the films—all that makes her crazy. She just rents everything she wants to see. She and Dad rent two or three films a week, taking turns making the selections since they don't always like the same ones. They bought a big-screen TV and a good surround sound system, and they would rather just stay home than bother with theater crowds."

"Sounds like a good plan to me."

"Do your parents see many movies?"

"They actually prefer live theater. Mother's been known to complain about the behavior of modern theater patrons. She misses the days when everyone got dressed up and made going to the theater a special occasion."

"I haven't seen many plays since Laurie quit acting in high school and college performances," Mike admitted. "Seemed like all the plays she was in were either just endless, boring talk scenes or incredibly depressing stories about somebody dying tragically."

Amused, Catherine turned in the truck seat to look at him as he drove them home from the movie theater. "You never saw any plays that you liked?"

"Well, yeah. A couple. I like the musicals. *Fiddler on the Roof* was my favorite. And *Guys and Dolls* was okay. That 'Luck Be a Lady' song? I like that one."

It surprised her a bit that he liked musicals, and she told him so.

"Well, yeah. I mean, I'd rather see people singing and dancing than philosophizing and dying dramatically, you know?"

She laughed. "Actually, I like musicals, myself, though I also enjoy the more dramatic plays." She hesitated only a moment before saying, "The local community theater is putting on *Seven Brides for Seven Brothers* next weekend. Karen and I were going to go, but then she found out that Wayne's brother from Chicago is going to be in town then, so I've ended up with an extra ticket. I was going to ask Julia, but if you're interested, maybe you'd like to—?"

"I'd like that," he said quickly. "Thanks for asking."

She didn't know if he was really interested in seeing the play or if he just wanted the excuse to see her again. Either way, she was pleased that he'd accepted. And maybe a little nervous about it, too. After all, they had just committed to spend another weekend together. And something—perhaps that same annoying inner voice that had nagged her the night before—warned her that the more time she spent with Mike, the harder it was going to be when they inevitably went their own ways.

Catherine and Mike saw each other nearly every day that week, and when they didn't get together, they spoke by phone. It was a light week at work for Catherine, so she had time to spend with him. As for him, he kept telling her that his classes were going well and he was keeping up with his studies. Other than that, they continued to pretend the rest of the world didn't exist.

This couldn't last, she reminded herself frequently. They were ignoring their friends and his family. She hadn't even mentioned him to her parents. They were also pretty much ignoring the differences between them.

They limited their activities to the very few things they had already tried successfully. They went for long walks along the scenic hiking trail that ran alongside the Arkansas River. They played board games and card games. They watched television when they could find programs that were of some interest to both of them. They dined out at rather generic chain restaurants where both could find dishes they liked. They played with Norman, and they enjoyed each other.

Catherine had never been in a physical relationship that was so intense. Mike was passionate and demonstrative, making no secret of his desire for her. It was a heady feeling to walk across a room and know that he was watching appreciatively. As much as she valued being admired for her competence and intelligence, it was kind of nice to be on the receiving end of a handsome, virile young man's—well, lust, she thought with a warmth in her cheeks.

So maybe it would all burn out very quickly, and both of them would go back to the lives they had led before their chance meeting. Every woman should have memories of at least one exciting, impetuous affair to savor in her later years, right?

They both enjoyed the play they saw on Saturday evening. Had she attended with Karen, as originally planned, Catherine might have been a bit more critical later of the individual actors and the directorial decisions, but since Mike had seemed satisfied with the production, she kept those opinions to herself. After all, she had liked the play, she assured herself. She was simply in the habit of critically reviewing plays and films afterward with her companions.

Mike's review of the play was succinct. "That was fun. And the actress who played Milly was hot."

Taking her cue from him, she agreed that the production had been enjoyable, then added teasingly, "I didn't really notice that actress so much—but the guy who played Benjamin was definitely hot."

"Oh, yeah?" Standing in the middle of her

living room, he wrapped his arms around her, his eyes twinkling down into hers. "Hotter than me?"

She walked her fingers up his chest and gazed up at him through her lashes, giving him what she hoped was a coyly seductive smile. "Impossible," she murmured. "But about that actress—"

His lips hovering only a millimeter above hers, he asked, "What actress?"

Satisfied, she pulled his mouth to hers.

Norman had to be content with entertaining himself in the living room for quite a while that evening.

"A pathogenic fungus invades a plant. The infected plant produces what in response to the attack?"

"Have I ever told you how pretty you look in green?"

"Mike—what does the infected plant produce in response to the attack?"

Stretched out on her couch with his head in her lap and her cat on his stomach, Mike sighed. "Phytochrome."

"Very good." She popped a red M&M into his mouth as a reward. He grinned and chewed.

Setting the bowl of candies back on the end table beside her, she glanced at the study sheet in her hand. "Name two plant hormones that might be used to enhance stem elongation and fruit growth."

He sighed again, drawing her attention back to him. She almost sighed herself. He looked so darned good sprawled beside her, his long legs encased in faded jeans with a hole in the right knee, his feet in white socks, his blue plaid cotton shirt untucked and unbuttoned enough to reveal a mouthwatering expanse of sleek, tanned chest. His head was heavy on her thigh, his warmth seeping through the thin black athletic pants she wore with her lime green long-sleeved T-shirt.

It took her a moment to remember what she had asked him. "Mike, are you listening to me? Which plant hormones might be used to enhance stem elongation and fruit growth?"

"I heard you," he muttered, shifting his weight

a little and almost distracting her all over again. "Auxins and…some other one."

"Giberellins," she supplied patiently for him. "Describe the function of auxin."

"I haven't the foggiest idea." He reached up to draw her head down to his for a kiss. "But I do know that you have the prettiest eyes…"

"No." She pulled her lips from his with an effort. "You're supposed to be studying. You have a test."

"I'll study later. I need a break now."

"A break?" She glanced pointedly at his lazily reclined position. "From *what?*"

"From thinking. My brain is tired. Let's go for a walk."

"It's pouring rain outside."

"Is it?" He frowned, listened for a moment to the rain that had starting pounding steadily against the windows only a few minutes earlier, then made a face. "Okay. Then let's do something else. How do you feel about bowling?"

"I haven't bowled since a school field trip when I was in the eighth grade. I was lousy at it. My friends called me the queen of the gutter ball."

"I could give you some pointers. I'm pretty good."

She had no doubt of that. Mike seemed to be good at everything he did—with the exception of concentrating on his studying today. "Auxin acts by increasing the plasticity of the cell wall. You should remember that in case it's on the test."

"And I will," he said, a little impatiently now. He set Norman gently on the floor and swung his legs around to sit up. "I have plenty of time to get ready for the test. But you and I have only a few hours to spend together today, since you have to go into the lab this evening. Let's not waste our time with this stuff. I'll study after you go to work."

He'd had a little trouble understanding why she had to go into the lab at 8:00 p.m. and would probably be there until midnight. It pretty much took another scientist to comprehend the tricky timing of most experiments.

She set his study sheet aside. If he didn't want

to study for his test, she certainly had no right to nag him. She wasn't his mother.

"Okay," she said, "we'll do something else. But do we really want to go out into that pouring rain?"

He was already putting on his shoes. "You have an umbrella, don't you? We'll only be out long enough to get to the car and then into the bowling alley."

"You really want to go bowling?"

"Sure, why not? It's something active we can do inside. It'll be fun. I'll even buy you some nachos."

Setting aside her reservations about his studies and her disinclination to go out in the rainstorm, she compromised. Again. "I'll get my jacket and my umbrella. But I have to be back by seven."

"No problem," he assured her with a grin that was just a shade too close to smug.

"So. Dude. When are you going to rejoin the living?" Bob asked, sounding disgruntled.

Speaking into the headset that allowed him to keep his hands free while using his cell phone,

Mike tightened a screw on the new showerhead he was installing in a recently vacated apartment. "I've just been busy, Bob. Work, classes—"

"A certain sexy scientist."

The screwdriver slipped a little. Mike quickly corrected it. "Yeah, I've seen Catherine a few times."

Which translated to every chance he got, he added silently. And even that didn't seem like nearly enough, which worried him more than a little.

"You haven't hung out with Brandon and me for the past couple of weeks. Every time we've called, you've had other plans. We're sensitive guys, you know. We could get our tender feelings hurt."

Mike chuckled, as Bob expected, but he knew his friend wasn't entirely joking. He'd been hearing much the same things from his mother and sisters, whom he had been avoiding lately.

"So how about this afternoon? Want to meet us at Jolly's for some wings and beer?"

As it happened, Catherine would be working

late that day; she had said she probably wouldn't be home before eight. He had told her that wouldn't be a problem because he had to study. He had not just one, but two tests tomorrow. Both of his classes.

"I guess I could join you for a little while. But I can't stay long, Bob. I've got to study."

"Oh, sure, no problem. We'll just hang out for a little while. You can hit the books later."

Even as they disconnected the call, Mike was aware that Bob had brushed off the studying as unimportant. Which meant it was going to be up to him to make sure he got away at a reasonable time, he told himself firmly.

"How about meeting for sushi this evening?" Julia asked Catherine over the phone in Catherine's office. "We haven't done anything together since we went shopping last month."

Catherine set down the pen she'd been using to write in her lab notebook. "I'm sorry, Julia, but I'll be working late this evening. I don't expect to be able to leave before eight—and it could be even later than that. It has been a very busy past couple of weeks here, and I've been putting in some fairly long hours."

"Working, huh?"

"Yes." Catherine spoke more firmly this time, having heard the faintest note of skepticism in Julia's voice. "Working."

"Okay—so how about tomorrow evening?"

Glad that Julia couldn't see her expression, Catherine thought about it a moment. Tomorrow was Friday, and Mike had classes. "Yes, I'm free tomorrow evening."

"So you're not still seeing that guy?" Julia didn't have to specify which guy.

"If you mean Mike, yes, I'm still seeing him quite often. But he and I have no plans for tomorrow night."

Julia had to have heard the note of warning in Catherine's voice, but she didn't back off. "You're sleeping with him, aren't you?"

Catherine allowed her silence to provide all the answer Julia was going to get.

"Look, I know you're thinking that this is

none of my business, but I just have to warn you again to be careful. I know this is all heady and exciting right now, but just keep your defenses up, okay? You've made a good life for yourself. You're one of the most confident and well-adjusted people I know. You seemed pretty content with who you are and what you've accomplished. I hope you don't let this affair change any of that."

Had Catherine not taken a moment to remind herself how badly Julia had been hurt, she might have lost her precarious grip on her patience then. She wanted to snap at her friend that she didn't need to be given advice on her relationship with Mike. But she kept those comments to herself. Partly because she knew Julia was genuinely concerned. And maybe another part of her was aware that the wisdom Julia had gained through painful experience could prove to be very useful soon.

"I appreciate your concern," she said eventually, choosing her words with care. "But I'll be fine, Julia. Mike and I are just having a little fun, you know? I know better than to take it seriously."

"Well, as long as you're not getting too emotionally invested," Julia said doubtfully. "Because, you know, guys like that don't tend to hang around long. They have very short attention spans."

"I know." In fact, Catherine suspected that Mike was already getting restless.

He was a very social person, comfortable in crowds and at parties. They had been avoiding their friends because it just seemed easier to do so than to deal with the complications. It was entirely possible that Mike was getting tired of spending hours in her apartment—which would explain his eagerness to go bowling last Sunday afternoon, even if it meant dashing through a downpour to get to her car.

He had seemed to enjoy the outing. He liked bowling—an active sport performed in a noisy venue with lots of other people around. He seemed to be energized by the noise and bustle, and thrived on competition, even against her pitiful attempts at knocking down the pins. He had been visibly disappointed when she had told him it was time to leave so that she could go to work.

She hoped he had studied that evening, as he had said he would, but she had promised herself she wouldn't ask him about it—and she had not, even though she'd seen him a couple of times since, and had talked to him almost every day by telephone.

"It's just a fling, Julia," she said, shaking her head to rid herself of the uncomfortable musings. "I don't expect it to last much longer, but there's no reason I shouldn't enjoy it while it does. Right?"

"I suppose not. But you shouldn't let him drive a wedge between you and your old friends, either. After all, we're the ones who will still be here after he gets bored and moves on."

She made it sound so inevitable. And so imminent. Not exactly flattering.

Catherine murmured an appropriate response, then agreed to meet Julia for dinner Friday evening, suggesting they invite Karen, as well. She might as well face both of her friends in one evening, though she sincerely hoped they wouldn't spend the entire time lecturing her about how Mike was probably going to break her heart.

Chapter Thirteen

Mike sat with Bob and Brandon at a table in a downtown club. They had already consumed baskets of buffalo wings and potato skins and fried mushrooms and several beers apiece. Music blared out of speakers all around them, and the mostly young crowd at surrounding tables did their best to converse above the noise. The place smelled like smoke and grease and people, and Mike felt right at home there.

Though it hadn't been that long since he had last seen them, it was good to be with his friends again in one of their favorite hangouts. He knew quite a few other patrons in the club, at least in passing, and he spent much of the evening returning friendly nods and greetings. This wasn't a place he thought Catherine would like very much, so he didn't know why he couldn't get her out of his mind.

"Mike—look who's here," Brandon said, tugging at the sleeve of Mike's shirt. "It's Jessica Terry. And, dude, she is totally checking you out."

Mike glanced in the direction Brandon was not-so-discreetly indicating to where a curvy blonde sat beside an equally striking woman with long black hair. Both were looking their way, and the blonde smiled brightly when Mike's gaze met hers.

Jessica Terry. He had met her at a party in September and had left with every intention of calling her—and then he'd met Catherine and had forgotten all about Jessica. The way she was looking at him, along with the open invitation in her eyes, suggested that she remembered him.

"Hey, I remember her," Bob said. "She was at Joey's party, wasn't she? Oh, man, she's hot. And as I recall, you and she did a little making out before that party was over. You probably would have ended up taking her home if she hadn't, you know, been there with some other guy."

Oh, yeah, Mike remembered. He had left that party with her number in his pocket and an ache that a cold shower had barely taken the edge off. Funny how he could look at her now and feel nothing. Zip. Nada.

He nodded to her and turned his attention back to his companions. "Are there any more potato skins?"

"Why don't you ask them over?" Bob suggested, pushing a hand through his shaggy red hair in a futile effort to tame it. "You can have Jessica and I'll take the brunette."

"Hey!" Brandon protested. "What about me?"

"Didn't I let you have the cheerleader at Laurie's Halloween party?" Bob returned. "It's my turn, dude."

"That doesn't count," Brandon argued. "That didn't last past the second dance."

"Not my problem."

"Let me solve this one," Mike suggested. "You guys can have them both. Decide between you who hits on which one. You're both going to strike out, of course, but I guess there's no harm in taking a shot."

Both of his friends turned to stare at him. "Are you kidding me?" Bob asked. "It's you she's looking at, man."

"Yeah, well, I'm not interested tonight."

Complete silence met that announcement. He glanced up defensively. "What? I told you I've got to study tonight."

"You're going back to your apartment—alone—to do homework, when Jessica Terry is sitting there practically waving you over?" Brandon asked in disbelief.

"It's not homework. I've got tests tomorrow. Two of them."

"Big deal. You'll either pass or you won't. This is Jessica-freakin'-Terry," Bob grumbled. "And she's with a friend. A smoking-hot friend."

"No, I can't. Not tonight. I told you when you

called that I have to leave early." And he had already missed that goal, he thought with a frowning glance at his watch. It was almost nine o'clock already.

"This isn't like you, Mike," Brandon said. "What's going on?"

Mike's cell phone rang before he could reply. He pulled it out of his pocket, glanced at the caller ID readout, and suppressed a wince. "Hi," he said, holding the phone to his ear and turning slightly away from his companions.

"Mike? I can hardly hear you," Catherine said. "You asked me to call you when I got home from work. I just got in."

He had forgotten about making that request. At the time, he'd expected to be alone in his apartment with his textbooks when she called. He had thought chatting with her would provide a pleasant and well-deserved break. "How did your experiment go?"

"Not particularly well. Some of the plates were contaminated. Do you have your radio turned up that loud or are you—"

"Hi, Mike. I've been trying to get your attention over there," Jessica Terry said with a little pout, leaning over the table to give him an eyeful of creamy cleavage. "Aren't you even going to say hi?"

If a cell phone could suddenly turn cold in one's hand, Mike's did at that moment. "Apparently, I've called at a bad time," Catherine said.

"No," he said, motioning for Bob and Brandon to run interference with Jessica. "I was just having a quick drink with Bob and Brandon."

"I'm sorry, Mike, I can't really hear you. I'll let you get back to your friends. Good luck on your tests tomorrow."

She disconnected without giving him a chance to respond.

"Damn it," he said, snapping the phone shut and shoving it into his pocket. Throwing some money on the table, he pushed his chair back from the table. "I've got to go, guys. Jessica, it was nice to see you again."

Jessica looked a bit shocked that he was brushing her off so brusquely—and considering their previous encounter, he supposed he didn't blame her. Bob and Brandon were scowling.

"Boy," Brandon muttered. "She's got you jumping when she snaps her fingers, doesn't she? I never thought I'd see that."

"Look, I've just got to study, okay?" Mike repeated wearily. "I'll call you guys later."

He knew they weren't satisfied with his explanation. He didn't like leaving them annoyed with him, even though he was defensively aware that he was in the right this time. He had told them from the beginning that he couldn't stay long.

He was also troubled by his phone conversation with Catherine. He shouldn't be feeling this guilty. Yeah, he had asked her to call him, but he hadn't promised to stay at home all night waiting for the phone to ring. And, okay, he had told her he would be studying, but he hadn't said he wouldn't take a break for a while. He hadn't known then that his friends would call and ask him to join them for a drink.

As for Jessica, it wasn't as if he had done any more than nod at her. And even if he *had* done more, he and Catherine didn't have any sort of exclusive arrangement. They were both free to see other people—though the thought of her doing so made his knuckles go white around the steering wheel.

This was getting way more difficult than he had anticipated. If he had any sense at all, he would get out before it became even more complicated.

Catherine was still fuming some time after she had abruptly hung up on Mike.

"It isn't as if I care if he's out drinking and flirting," she assured Norman as she paced restlessly through her apartment with her pet following curiously at her heels. "I certainly don't tell him where he can go or what he can do when he isn't with me."

Norman meowed.

"Exactly," she agreed emphatically. "I wasn't trying to check up on him. I didn't particularly care if he was home or not. I was actually too tired to talk on the phone, anyway. But he *asked* me to call him when I got home."

Not to mention that he had told her flat-out that he would be studying for two tests tomorrow. Maybe he had fully intended to follow that itinerary and had joined his friends on an impulse. He certainly had the right to do so.

"It's no skin off my nose if he fails one or both of his tests," she told Norman loftily.

He made a sound that might have expressed skepticism of her claim of disinterest.

"And I don't care how many people are sitting in his lap right now trying to get his attention," she added, growing indignant all over again.

She caught a glimpse of herself in a mirror, and the sight brought her up short. What was she doing, pacing around and ranting like a mad woman? Her eyes were glinting, her cheeks were flushed, her teeth were all but bared in anger.

Shoulders sagging, she pushed her hands through her hair and ordered herself to calm down. This was ridiculous. It really *wasn't* any of her business where Mike was or what he was doing right now. They certainly had no exclusive arrangement, nor did either of them want that sort of commitment.

They had just been having fun. A no-strings fling. Weren't those the exact words she had used to reassure Julia that she wasn't getting too involved with Mike? That she wasn't going to end up hurting and emotionally bruised when it ended?

Her doorbell rang, and she stiffened again. She was pretty certain she knew who was at her door at this late hour. What she didn't know was why he was here.

Mike's expression was grim when Catherine opened the door. Almost angry, for some reason.

"It's late," she said, "and I'm tired."

"This won't take long."

He waited implacably on the doorstep until she sighed and moved back to allow him to enter. She could smell the faint scents of smoke and beer as he passed, reminding her that he had been at a club only a short time earlier. Closing the door behind him, she asked, "Why are you here?"

"You said you couldn't hear me on the phone earlier," he replied, turning to face her. "Can you hear me now?"

Lifting her chin, she decided not to answer that rather testy question.

"I was trying to tell you that nothing was going on," he continued. "I had some food and a couple of drinks with Bob and Brandon. There was a girl at the club I'd met once at a party, but I hadn't even spoken to her when you called."

"You don't owe me explanations," she told him, pushing her hands into the pockets of her khaki slacks.

"You know, that's what I told myself all the way home. And then I reminded myself that I'd told you I would be studying all evening."

"Plans change," she said with a shrug intended to look nonchalant. "Your friends called, and you joined them. I understand."

"I told them I had to leave early to study, but every time I tried to get away, they made me feel all guilty and defensive."

Remembering the way Julia had done pretty

much the same thing to her that afternoon, Catherine softened just a little. "I understand. But really, Mike, you didn't have to come here tonight."

"I didn't like the way our phone call ended," he said, searching her face. "I didn't like the way I felt after you hung up."

She wished now that she had never called in the first place. She had hesitated before doing so, but she had thought he might have a question about his biology studies. And besides, she reminded herself yet again, he had asked her to call. "I didn't mean to ruin your evening."

"You didn't ruin my evening. I was ready to leave, anyway."

He looked so serious. Almost anxious. Probably, he had been having fun with his friends, whom he certainly hadn't seen much lately. Despite what he said, hearing her annoyed voice on his cell phone had obviously put an end to the evening for him.

She didn't like to think of herself as a killjoy. And she *really* hated being seen as some sort of mother figure, nagging him to study for his tests.

"Maybe I'm just too tired, but I'm not sure what you came here to say."

He raised a hand to brush her hair back from her face. His smile looked as weary as she felt—but the expression in his eyes made her knees go weak. "I just wanted to see you tonight. I missed you."

She reached up to catch his hand and hold it against her cheek. She couldn't think of anything at all to say—and she wasn't sure she could have pushed the words past the lump in her throat, anyway—so she just stood there, gazing up at him.

He bent his head and brushed a kiss across her lips. A little shiver ran through her, and she rested both hands against his chest, her fingers curling slightly into the fabric of his shirt.

The next kiss wasn't nearly as fleeting or tentative. Wrapping both arms around her, he pulled her close and covered her mouth with his again. More firmly this time. More confidently, as if he were a bit more assured that his embrace would be welcomed.

Just in case he still had any doubt about that, she slid her arms around his neck and parted her lips for him. The kiss deepened, and their hearts began to pound against each other. Maybe they sometimes had a little trouble communicating with words, she thought somewhat dazedly, but they had no trouble connecting in this way.

It wasn't enough—but it would do for now.

Mike was drawing her toward the bedroom when she suddenly came to her senses. "Wait. We can't do this."

"Sure we can," he said, taking another step toward the bedroom. "And we do it very well, I might add."

She might have heartily agreed with that sentiment, had she not been clinging so determinedly to her willpower.

"You have those tests tomorrow."

"I know the material," he assured her. "Haven't you told me you don't approve of night-before-the-test cramming?"

"It's not as effective as daily studying, but—"

He moved closer to her and toyed suggestively

with the top button of her blouse. "I'll do better on my tests if I'm relaxed and feeling good."

Looking at him with reproach, she said, "That's a very weak argument."

He chuckled, and the button slid smoothly out of its hole. "Sorry. It was the best I could come up with on short notice."

"You really should—"

"Catherine." His wandering hands stilled as he looked her in the eyes. "Forget the tests for now. If you want me to go, just say so."

This was the point where she should insist that he go home and study for his exams. But because she was still smarting over that mental image of herself as a crabby chaperone, she decided she would do no such thing. Mike didn't need her to fret about his grades. He was certainly old enough to make his own decisions about such things.

Instead she responded specifically to what he had said. "I don't want you to go."

He grinned and pulled her into his arms again. He wasn't worried about the tests, so she wouldn't either, she promised herself. She could be as relaxed and impulsive as the next person. She could be like his other friends, the ones he'd been hanging out with until she had called and ruined his evening.

If there were any lingering misgivings—and there were—she pushed them very firmly to the back of her mind.

Mike left Catherine early the next morning, saying he would shower and change for work in his own apartment. She walked him to the door. "I'm having dinner with Julia and Karen this evening."

"Tell them hello for me."

"I will. I hope your day goes well." She deliberately left the wish vague, choosing not to mention his tests.

"Thanks. Yours, too. Good luck with that, uh, contamination problem."

They hadn't talked much about the specifics of her job. He hadn't asked many questions—whether from lack of real interest or discomfort with discussing highly technical scientific procedures, she wasn't certain. And because she was so accustomed to nonscientists looking bored when she talked about her work, she hadn't brought it up very often, herself. She was actually a bit surprised that he even remembered her mentioning the contamination problem during their brief, awkward conversation when he was at the club with his friends.

"Thanks," she said. "I'll work it out."

He started to reach for the doorknob, then paused and looked at her. "So, we're good?"

She wasn't sure exactly what he meant, but it seemed safe enough to smile and say, "We're good."

He kissed her quickly, then drew back to smile at her. "I'll see you tomorrow, okay?"

"Call me in the morning and we'll make arrangements. I have to go into the lab for an hour or so, but I'm free after that."

After he left, Catherine sank bonelessly onto her couch and picked up Norman, stroking him mechanically.

For an affair that was supposed to be "just for fun"—just a lighthearted fling—this was beginning to feel entirely too serious. Too many of her emotions were becoming involved, and she could not even define most of them.

Maybe she had better start paying attention to Julia's pessimistic warnings and cynical advice, after all.

"What are your plans for Thanksgiving?" Karen asked during dinner that evening, addressing the question to both Julia and Catherine.

Julia answered first. "I'm flying to Miami to spend Thanksgiving with my parents. We're all going to Colorado for Christmas with my brother, so it looks as though my holidays are booked."

"What about you, Catherine?" Karen inquired.

Catherine shrugged. "Since my parents aren't going to be in the country, I haven't made any plans. I'll probably just spend the day relaxing."

Karen shook her head emphatically. "There's no need for you to spend the day alone. I'm thinking about cooking a big, traditional Thanksgiving dinner now that I finally have a kitchen big enough to accommodate everything. It's silly to cook that much just for Wayne and myself, so I'd like to invite a few people to join us. Bonnie and Chris, of course, and you."

Catherine wasn't usually enthusiastic about spending holidays with other people's families, but this was a group she wouldn't mind so much. "That sounds nice."

Her expression turning speculative, Karen asked, "How would you feel if I invite Bill James?"

Catherine scowled. "Karen—"

"Well, this is his first Thanksgiving since his mother died. He doesn't have any other family, so he's going to be alone for the holiday."

"Since when do you know so much about him?"

"I run into him in the hallways fairly often, since he does some research in my department. He and I happened to be in the coffee shop at the same time last week, and we shared a table for a few minutes while we had our coffee and muffins."

"And all you talked about was the upcoming holiday season?" Catherine asked suspiciously.

"Your name might have come up."

Catherine groaned.

"It was no big deal," Karen assured her hastily. "He just mentioned that he knew you and I are good friends and he asked how you are. I said you'd been really busy with work and he said he'd already figured that out because he's hardly seen you lately. And then he said he hoped your schedule would slow down enough so that you can have dinner with him again soon."

"And you encouraged him to call me, didn't you?" Catherine accused.

"I might have said something like that."

"Karen—"

"What? You said he's a really nice guy and you had a good time with him at Dr. McNulty's retirement party."

"He is, and I did. But that doesn't mean I want to go out with him again."

"Right," Julia murmured. "Why would you

want to go out with a mature, settled guy with a real job and a solid future?"

"Okay, here's the rule," Catherine said, turning on Julia. "You don't talk about Mike—even indirectly—tonight, and I won't remind you that you slept with Buzz Stewart."

Julia's face went bright red, and she quickly went back to eating her dinner. Satisfied that she had effectively silenced Julia for a while—no small accomplishment—Catherine turned back to Karen. "You certainly have the right to invite anyone you like to your Thanksgiving dinner, but I really wish you would stop trying to fix me up with Bill. I'm just really not interested right now."

"Since I *didn't* sleep with Buzz Stewart—*ew, by the way*—can *I* ask you about Mike?" Karen asked bravely.

"No."

"I really didn't know you were still seeing him," Karen said, anyway. "You haven't mentioned him at all."

Catherine could concede that point. She had very carefully avoided mentioning Mike to her friends. She was not ashamed of her relationship with him, she assured herself. The truth was, she just hadn't wanted to talk about it.

"So do you have plans for Thanksgiving with Mike?" Karen persisted.

"We haven't talked about Thanksgiving. I assume he'll be spending the holiday with his family." And since his sisters had disliked her at first sight, for some reason, she didn't imagine she would be on their list of preferred guests. Not that she wanted to be included, anyway. Talk about awkward. And she and Mike were nowhere near the point of spending holidays with each other's families.

"I'll come to your dinner party," she told Karen. "But I mean it, no matchmaking. Just treat Bill and me as friends and colleagues, nothing more."

"Isn't that what you said about—"

Catherine pointed a finger at Julia before she could finish the question. "Buzz Stewart."

Julia grimaced and reached grumpily for her wineglass. Karen snickered, though she quickly sobered when Julia gave her a look.

Firmly changing the subject, Catherine guided the conversation into a much more comfortable direction for the remainder of the meal.

Chapter Fourteen

Mike put his truck into Park and turned off the engine, then turned to smile at Catherine. "Well?"

She looked through the windshield at the tidy little lakefront cottage to which he had driven her. "It's very nice."

And she still found it hard to believe she was there. That Mike had talked her into an impulsive weekend trip to a friend's lakeside cabin an hour's drive southwest of Little Rock.

They had left her apartment at ten o'clock on this Saturday morning before Thanksgiving, and planned to return sometime late the next afternoon. Since he had suggested the outing only a couple of days before, Catherine had found it necessary to scramble a bit to clear her calendar, but somehow she had managed.

Mike was a very persuasive guy, she thought in bemusement as she climbed out of the truck and reached behind the seat for her overnight bag. She couldn't imagine anyone else who could have talked her into going away with him for the weekend, especially on such short notice.

The weather was cool but clear. A light denim jacket with a thin red sweater and jeans were all she needed to stay comfortable. Overhead the sky was deep blue and almost cloudless. The fall leaves were almost all gone now, but there were plenty of evergreens around, and the glittering lake was tinted with blues and greens and silver.

"It really is lovely here."

Mike paused on the front porch, key in hand, to glance toward the lake. "It's great, isn't it? This place has been in my friend Dan's family for a long time. He took possession of it when his parents retired to Arizona a couple of years ago. A group of us comes here in the summers sometimes to drink beer and water-ski and play poker until dawn."

"I'm sure you enjoy that."

"Oh, yeah." He led her into the cabin and dropped his own bag on the floor so he could turn on the lights. "He didn't mind letting us have the place tonight, since it isn't used so much in the winter."

He went back out to the truck to bring in the food they had brought with them after stopping at a nearby grocery store. During the few minutes that he was gone, Catherine looked around the small cabin. The open floor plan made it look somewhat larger. She stood in the main room, which was painted a warm taupe, floored in age-buffed wood, furnished in sturdy oak furniture with nubby plaid upholstery and anchored by a large brick fireplace on one side.

The back wall was mostly glass, giving a view of a wooden deck on the back of the cabin and the lake beyond. The efficient-looking kitchen was visible behind a long, granite eating bar lined with four tall bar stools. Two closed doors on the other side of the room presumably led into bedrooms and bathroom facilities. The overall effect was ultracasual comfort, a place for kicking off one's shoes and ignoring the outside world.

Mike walked back in carrying several bulging plastic grocery bags. "What do you think?"

"It's perfect. I'll put the groceries away while you take our bags into the bedroom."

He came out of the bedroom again rubbing his hands together as if in anticipation. "Want to go for a boat ride?"

She turned away from the well-appointed kitchen to ask, "There's a boat?"

"Yeah. It's in the boathouse next to the dock. Dan's taking it out next week to store it for the rest of the winter, but he gave us permission to use it this weekend."

"I, er, suppose you know how to drive it."

"No, but between us, we can probably figure it out." Laughing at her expression, he shook his head. "I've been operating boats since I was ten—and I've driven Dan's more times than I can remember. You'll be perfectly safe."

"Then let's go."

"Wait—before we go, you'd better put on a hat. Your denim jacket will probably be warm enough, especially under the life vest, but your head might get cold from the wind in the boat."

So that was why he had insisted she bring a knit cap, along with a heavier coat in case they wanted to sit outside after sundown. It was a mild weekend. Winter weather didn't usually set in until mid to late December in Arkansas, so they could expect comfortable temperatures for the next two days.

"A little too cold for water-skiing, though," Mike said regretfully.

"Yes, I think so." Now wearing her red knit cap, she eyed the metallic blue boat in the boat-house with some trepidation. "It looks fast."

He gave her a grin that made her heart skip a beat. "Baby, it *is* fast."

Uncertain whether her racing pulse was due more to nerves or to Mike himself, Catherine took his outstretched hand and stepped into the boathouse.

Mike assisted her into a life jacket, his head close to hers as he helped her fasten the front snaps. Their hands tangled at the task, and for a moment he paused just to hold her hands and smile at her. She smiled back up at him, and she was dimly aware that this was one of those perfect moments she would treasure for the rest of her life.

"Catherine?"

"Mmm?"

"You sit in that seat. I'll push us off."

Blinking, she returned abruptly to reality. Looking in the direction he had indicated, she nodded and let him help her into the boat.

Mike didn't remember ever seeing Catherine quite so relaxed as she was that afternoon. They'd had a very pleasant boat ride, during which he had been on his best behavior behind the wheel. The wind had whipped color into her cheeks, until they were almost as red as her cap. Her eyes had gleamed with pleasure as she had pointed out birds and other wildlife they passed during their cruise around the lake.

He had talked her into taking the wheel, and after her initial hesitation, she'd seemed to enjoy piloting a boat for the first time. And then she had turned the wheel back over to him and simply sat back in her seat to enjoy the remainder of the ride.

They had lunch after returning to the cabin, turkey and cheese sandwiches on whole wheat bread with raw baby carrots and yogurt dip. Catherine had chosen the menu. He probably would have just grabbed some bologna and crackers. He had to admit the lunch she had put together was better.

She was the one who suggested a walk after lunch. They strolled along the road that ran next to the lake, stopping occasionally to admire a particularly interesting sight. A rock shiny with embedded quartz. A squirrel busily digging up something buried beneath a big oak tree. Tiny fish darting through the water lapping at the gravel bank.

At some point during their stroll, it just seemed natural to reach out and take her hand. Their fingers interlaced as comfortably as if they had been walking this way for years.

He tried to analyze what he was feeling at that moment, but he could come up with only one word. *Peaceful.* There was no stress, no pressure, no reason to try to be anything other than himself. No other people around to come between them or remind them of their separate lives. There was just the easy contentment of being with Catherine.

Part of him wished he could hold on to this moment forever. Another part of him was aware that he would miss his family. His friends. His life.

They had reached a small playground area, where several others were taking advantage of the nice afternoon. Three women sat on a bench chatting while five children ranging in age from toddlers to perhaps eight or nine played on the slide and swings and climbing tower.

Mike grinned as a little boy launched himself down the slide with a yell. "Man, remember how it felt to be that free and unconcerned about anything beyond the moment?"

She watched two little girls chase each other playfully around a colorful plastic horse mounted on a heavy spring for rocking. "It's hard to remember ever being that young."

"So, were you one of those serious kids who never cut loose and played?"

She lifted an eyebrow, then nodded toward the climbing tower. "I'll have you know I'd have been at the top of that tower in a heartbeat. I *was* Supergirl."

"Supergirl, huh?" He was greatly intrigued by that revelation. "That was your childhood hero?"

"Well, Supergirl and Marie Curie."

He grinned, delighted with the image. "Comic books?"

"Oh, definitely. My father bought them for me and smuggled them into the house when Mother wasn't looking. I had a red towel that was my 'cape' and I begged for a pair of red boots. Mother couldn't imagine where I got all those silly ideas."

There was a smile in her eyes as the memories crossed her face. She was obviously more amused than annoyed by her mother's quirks, which showed that the family had been close despite their oddities. As different as Catherine's family had been from his own, he could identify with the closeness—and with the fond exasperation over a strict mother's sometimes capricious rules.

He was absolutely enthralled with the mental picture of a pint-size Catherine in a red towel and red boots. "Superhero to scientist," he murmured. "Interesting metamorphosis."

"Some would say it's an oxymoron."

Chasing a runaway ball, a towheaded little boy of maybe five barreled across the playground and nearly crashed into Mike's legs. Mike steadied himself quickly and caught the kid's shoulders before the boy went over backward. "You okay, sport?"

"Uh-huh. Will you throw me the ball?"

Grinning, Mike reached down to pick up the ball. "Okay. Go long."

Proving that sports were already a part of his life, the boy started running, looking back expectantly at Mike. Mike drew back his arm and lobbed the ball neatly into the kid's grasp. The boy whooped victoriously and dashed off again.

Mike turned back to Catherine, who was watching him with a smile. "You're good with kids," she said.

"I like kids. I told you, I'm cool Uncle Mike."

They turned back toward the cabin, their steps matching automatically. "I always thought I would make a good aunt. You know, the kind who gives books and chemistry sets for Christmas gifts? But since my parents neglected to provide me with siblings, I suppose I'll never know."

"You could always marry into some," he quipped.

The lighthearted remark sort of hung in the air between them, then dropped heavily into awkward silence. Mike cleared his throat and hastily changed the subject. "Nice sailboat out there, isn't it? Have you ever done any sailing?"

"No, I haven't," she said entirely too

brightly. "I've always thought it looked interesting, though."

Relived that the sticky moment had passed, Mike started babbling about sailing.

Still, at the back of his mind he found himself thinking that Catherine would make a terrific aunt.

They sat outside after dinner, flames flickering in a fire bowl in front of their outdoor chairs. The temperature had dropped, and they had both donned heavier jackets. The warmth of the fire felt good against Catherine's cheeks. She sighed and stretched her feet toward the bowl, warming her toes through her boots.

"We should have thought to buy some marshmallows," Mike said lazily, gazing into the flames.

"I'm not hungry, anyway." They had made spaghetti for dinner, using sauce from a jar, with frozen garlic rolls and premade salads on the side. Her tummy was still pleasantly full as she rocked gently in the wrought iron spring chair.

Moonlight sparkled over the lake ahead of her, and she could hear night birds calling in the distance. The scent of smoke tickled her nose. A car went by on the road behind them, the radio bass booming so loudly that she could almost feel the vibration in her teeth, but then it was gone and the night was peaceful again.

"Are you too cold?" Mike asked.

"No, I'm fine. The fire feels good."

"Yeah, it does." He reached down beside his chair, picked up a stick of wood and tossed it into the flames, adding another few degrees of warmth.

They sat in companionable silence for a little while longer. Catherine couldn't remember being this utterly relaxed in a very long time. She could almost go to sleep right there in her chair.

"It's been a nice day, hasn't it?"

She roused enough to respond. "It's been a wonderful day."

A few minutes later he chuckled.

"What?" she asked.

"Oh, I was just thinking about that kid we saw in the park today. He's a handful, I bet."

Remembering the boy's ear-piercing shrieks,

Catherine smiled. "No doubt about that. But he was cute, wasn't he?"

"Yeah. Reminded me of my oldest nephew."

"Is he a handful, too?"

"There are some who say he's a lot like me at that age."

Catherine wasn't at all fooled by his innocent tone. "Which means that he's a bit of a brat, right?"

Mike folded his hands over his stomach, his long legs stretched toward the fire. "I'd resent that if I could work up the energy."

"But you won't go to that trouble, because you know it's true."

"You're probably right. My mother says someday I'll have to pay for my raising when I have my own son."

He was laughing as he spoke, but the thought of Mike's son brought a nervous lump to her throat. She could almost picture a little blond version of him, and for some reason the image made her chest ache.

She quickly changed the subject. "You never

told me—did you ever register for your classes for next semester? What did you decide to take?"

Mike's smile faded so fast it was as if it had been wiped from his face. "I still haven't decided. I don't know if I even will take any classes next semester."

It was the first she'd heard that he was even considering dropping out again. The decision was entirely his, of course, and he had to decide what was best for him, but she couldn't help asking, "Why?"

He kept his gaze focused on the fire. "I don't know. It just seems sort of pointless. I mean— man, it's going to take years to finish. And I don't really have a major or anything…"

He sounded more discouraged than disinterested, she realized suddenly. Maybe he just needed a little encouragement. "You've talked before about taking more hours a semester, maybe getting finished a little more quickly."

"Yeah, but we'd still be talking about years. Do you know how old I'd be by then?"

"Only a couple of years older than I am now,"

she replied wryly. "And I'm not exactly ready for retirement, Mike."

She thought he flushed a little, but it was hard to tell in the firelight. "I didn't mean to imply that you are. It's just…"

"You're doing so well in your classes. It would be a shame to let the hard work you've put in this semester go to waste."

He was quiet for a notably long time before murmuring, "Actually, my grades have slipped a little."

Frowning, she turned to face him. "Since when? Your grades were very good the last time you talked to me about them."

"Those, uh, last two tests—I didn't do so great on either of them."

As she recalled, he had spent the night before those tests drinking with his friends, then making love with her. He'd had to work all day the next day, right up until time to leave for his classes. And since then, he had spent most of his spare time with her, assuring her that he was studying during the time they weren't together.

She would not accept guilt for this, she told herself firmly—despite the way that emotion tried to creep into her mind. She had done everything she could to get Mike to take his classes seriously. "I'm sure you can make up for those two exams by doing very well on your finals. But it's up to you, of course, what you do from this point."

"Disappointed in me?" He spoke lightly, but she sensed the sincerity behind the question.

She took a moment to phrase her answer. Speaking candidly, as she always had with him, she said, "I just don't want you to be disappointed in yourself. If you were only going to school to prove something to other people, then it wouldn't matter so much. But I thought you were going to prove something to yourself. And that makes me wonder if you aren't selling yourself short again."

"I know I can do it, if that's what you mean. I've proven to myself that I can keep my grades up if I work hard enough at it. But maybe I just don't want to spend the next four to six years working that hard."

"I understand that it seems daunting now. I've even been there myself. There were times during graduate school when I came very close to burnout. I felt as though I'd been in school all my life and that all I'd ever done was work and study while everyone else my age was out playing and enjoying their youth."

"And I was one of the ones out playing while you were working," he muttered. "Now you and the others who went straight through in school are settled into jobs and have the means to make plans for your future, and even take some time off occasionally."

She understood a little what he was trying to say, so she didn't bother to point out that this was the first weekend she had taken off in quite some time. She was still young, she still worked very hard, and she still had quite a way to go before she could consider herself secure and settled in her profession. But thinking of herself completely starting over again from early undergraduate studies was enough to make her almost shudder. Still…

"So what are you going to do if you quit?" she asked. "Will you continue to do maintenance work?"

"There's nothing wrong with maintenance work," he said defensively. "It's an honest living."

"And you do it very well," she responded mildly. "I didn't say there was anything wrong with your job—if it makes you feel fulfilled and content."

His silence made her suspect that he couldn't say either of those things. She remembered how happy his friend Bob seemed to be in his delivery job. Bob was doing exactly what he wanted to do, enjoying both his work and his life away from the job. Mike didn't seem to have that same satisfaction, which bothered her a great deal, because she wanted him to be happy.

He seemed to become aware of the lengthening silence between them. "I can't stay in this job indefinitely, of course. It doesn't pay much more than rent and necessities. It seemed like a good idea at the time, since it gave me time to take classes, but I need to find something with more chance for advancement. Something that doesn't require a master's degree," he added in a low voice.

She cocked her head, hearing more, perhaps, than he had intended to reveal in his words. "Was there something you were considering that does require a master's degree?"

"I thought maybe— But it doesn't matter. I've pretty much changed my mind."

It wasn't her business, she reminded herself. She shouldn't press him to talk. But, darn it, it wasn't as if they were just casual acquaintances. Surely they had progressed to a point where they could express genuine concern about each other. "What were you considering?"

He hesitated so long that she had begun to wonder if he was going to ignore her. Finally he said, "I thought about going into coaching and teaching at a middle school level. I mean, I like sports and kids, and my mom was a teacher for years, so I know what the job entails. But you really have to have a master's degree to get a good job in education."

"You would be a great teacher and coach," she said, struck by the image.

"Like I said, I've pretty much changed my mind."

"You're sure you want to do that? If it's just the time involved, you're only twenty-eight. You'd still be quite young by the time you finished your training. You'd have years to work before retirement. Do you want to reach that age and regret that you didn't pursue your dreams?"

"I never said it was my dream. It was just a passing thought. But really, Catherine, me as a teacher? Heck, I barely made it through high school, and pretty much flunked out of college the first time. It's kind of a joke, when you think about it."

"I'm not laughing," she said.

He fell silent.

There were so many more things she wanted to say. So many arguments she could make about why he should persevere. But maybe she had reached the limit of how much she could meddle.

The flames in the fire bowl were dying down,

and neither of them moved to put in more wood. The formerly comfortable, lazy air of companionship had been altered, leaving a subtle edge of tension between them. She regretted the change, and wondered if it was her fault.

"It's getting kind of cold out here," Mike said finally. "Ready to go in for hot chocolate?"

It was apparent that he didn't want to talk about his plans anymore just then. Catherine nodded obligingly, pushing herself out of her chair. They went inside together. Mike locked the door while she moved into the kitchen to heat water for the packets of instant cocoa they had brought with them.

She had just stirred the mix into two mugs of steaming water when Mike slipped his arms around her from behind. "Will you still go out with me even if I don't have a college degree?" he asked in her ear.

"You didn't have a college degree when I started seeing you," she replied matter-of-factly.

He chuckled. "You always have a candid answer for everything, don't you?"

"I try. Too bad we forgot marshmallows. We could have had some on our hot chocolate."

His voice was suddenly gruff as he turned her in his arms and lowered his head. "I don't want marshmallows. I want you."

"Then there's no problem, is there?" she responded, lifting her arms around his neck. "I'm right here."

Two mugs of cocoa grew cold on the counter, completely forgotten.

Chapter Fifteen

Catherine had mixed emotions when Mike turned into the parking lot of their apartment complex early Sunday evening. She was glad to be home, of course, and looking forward to seeing Norman again. And yet her weekend with Mike had been so nice, for the most part, that she almost regretted returning to their real lives and the problems that faced them.

And there were still problems. They could not keep avoiding their friends and his family. His indecision about what to do with his future was a bit of a sore point between them, one she felt compelled to discuss more intensely and which he had studiously avoided ever since their conversation by the fire last night.

"I'm sure Norman's going to be glad to see you," Mike said, turning off his truck engine.

"Are you kidding? He'll give me the cold shoulder. I'll have to grovel and apologize repeatedly, then give him double his usual salmon treats before he'll even acknowledge my presence. And then, after he has decided I'm properly chastened for daring to leave him overnight, even though I left him plenty of food and water and fresh litter and kitty toys, he'll deign to let me give him a tummy rub."

Mike laughed. "Norman has a way of making his feelings known, doesn't he?"

"Oh, yes. Norman communicates better than some people I know."

Mike helped her out of the truck, then carried her bag for her, waiting close behind her as she unlocked the door to her apartment. "Do you think Norman would let me say hi to him?"

She opened the door with a smile. "You can try."

Grinning, he accompanied her inside.

True to her prediction, Norman gave them one disdainful look, then sneered and pointedly turned his back to them, making Mike laugh again. "Oh, man, you are *really* going to have to crawl."

"Tell me about it." Smiling, she walked straight to the pantry for the salmon snacks.

Mike leaned a shoulder against a wall and watched as she coaxed Norman into a better mood. The cat was purring by the time she rose and went back into the kitchen to refill his food and water bowls. There was still a little dry kitty kibble in the food bowl, but she refilled it, anyway, just to keep him happy.

Hearing a sound behind her, she turned to see Mike standing in the doorway with Norman lying contently in his arms. "I apologized to him for taking you away for the weekend."

"I see he's forgiven you."

"Provisionally."

"You're lucky he made it so easy for you. Can I get you anything?"

"No, I'm good. Thanks." With a final pat to

Norman's head, he set the cat on the floor, then straightened.

Something about his expression caught Catherine's attention. She sensed that he was about to say something momentous, and a moment later he proved her right. "Catherine, will you come with me to my parents' house for Thanksgiving dinner?"

Startled, she said, "I, uh—what?"

"I know it's really short notice and maybe you already have other plans. We haven't talked about Thanksgiving because I wasn't sure how you would feel about me asking you. I know your first impression of my sisters wasn't very positive, but they really are nicer than they acted that night. I had a pretty good talk with both of them after the Halloween party, and they both admitted they didn't behave very well. I promise they'll be nice to you Thursday or red heads will roll."

While she was touched that he had asked, she had to shake her head. She would decide later whether she was relieved or disappointed that she had a legitimate reason to decline. "I'm sorry,

Mike, but I've already told Karen I would join her dinner party for Thanksgiving. It would be rude to rescind my acceptance at this late date."

He allowed his own disappointment to show on his face. "I'm sorry to hear that. I guess I should have risked asking you earlier."

"I really do appreciate the invitation."

"So Karen invited you to join her and Wayne for Thanksgiving?"

"Yes. She's having a, um, few people over for the holiday."

He must have noticed her slight hesitation. Or perhaps he read her expression a bit too well. "Who all will be there?"

She swallowed a sigh, suspecting he wasn't going to like her answer. "Karen and Wayne, of course. Bonnie and Chris. And Bill James."

Mike's eyes narrowed. "Bill James?"

"His mother died recently, and he has no other family in this area. Karen didn't want him to be alone for Thanksgiving."

"So she set him up with you?"

"It isn't a setup. She invited us both as friends

and colleagues who had no other plans for the holiday. There's nothing more to it."

"Does he know that?"

"I'm sure he does," she said, though she couldn't speak with the certainty he might have liked.

"Look, can't you get out of this? You could tell Karen that I've asked you to join my family for dinner. I'm sure she would understand."

Catherine lifted an eyebrow. "You think she would understand if I told her I'd changed my mind about joining them because I received a last-minute invitation from someone else?"

"Not just anyone else," he said defensively. "You and I are—well, you know."

"We're sleeping together. That doesn't change my obligation to my friend."

He didn't like that. His shoulders stiffened. "That's all this is between us? All it means to you?"

"I don't know what it is, exactly. We've had a good time together, but we've never discussed anything more. We haven't even known each other all that long, really."

"I thought we had progressed beyond counting the days since we met," he said stiffly.

"Mike, we haven't even been able to share our regular lives with each other. Your sisters don't approve of me for you, and you were bored half-senseless by my friends. It's entirely too soon for us to start defining a relationship."

"I'm sure Dr. Bill has much more in common with your friends."

Catherine's rare temper began to simmer. "Don't even go there."

"I can't help noticing that you've started hedging about our relationship since I told you I was thinking about dropping out of college again."

The simmer became a slow boil. "You are really starting to make me angry. I accepted this invitation days before I knew you were even considering not returning to school. You haven't even mentioned Thanksgiving until today. So you have absolutely no right to be annoyed that I've made other plans."

"You're correct, of course. I have no rights at all where you're concerned."

"Look, we've had a very nice weekend together. Let's not spoil it with a quarrel now."

"No, we wouldn't want to spoil anything, would we? Especially since we're only sleeping together."

She almost flinched. Instead, she lifted her chin and said, "Maybe we're both just tired. Or maybe you're under stress because you're having trouble deciding what you want to do with your life. But you have no reason to take that stress out on me."

"You know, maybe I should just take my tired, indecisive, stressed-out self out of your apartment before this turns ugly."

As far as she was concerned, it had already turned ugly. "Maybe you *should* go for tonight," she agreed. "We can talk again when we've both cooled off."

"Right." He turned on one heel to stalk toward the door. Throwing one last look back at her, he said, "Give my regards to all your doctor friends."

"I'll be sure and do that."

But he wasn't quite finished. "Is Dr. Bill

picking you up here? Maybe I should be here when he arrives, just to say hello."

One eyebrow rising, she responded in a chilly tone, "I don't think there's any chance of you running into him. That would involve you being somewhere on time for a change."

He spun on one heel and let himself out, leaving Catherine to indulge in a very rare bout of angry tears, followed by a restless night wondering how a perfect weekend could descend into such a stupid, bitter argument.

Mike shoved a forkful of turkey and dressing into his mouth and tried very hard to be thankful for it. No doubt about it, his mom was a great cook.

He wondered if Catherine was enjoying the meal Karen had prepared for her and Dr. Bill.

His family surrounded him. His parents, four sisters, two brothers-in-law, four children and two boyfriends. So it made no sense at all that what he seemed to be feeling was lonely.

His mother and sisters chattered like magpies

while the kids babbled and the men concentrated primarily on the food. If anyone had noticed that Mike was more subdued than usual, no one had commented as of yet.

Trust Laurie to bring up the one subject guaranteed to make his mood even darker. "I'm surprised you didn't bring your professor friend today. I thought you and she were pretty much joined at the hip lately."

"I told him he was welcome to bring a guest," Alice said when he didn't immediately respond. "I assume his friend had plans with her own family."

"Something like that," Mike muttered, jabbing his fork into a candied sweet potato.

"I would like to meet her," Alice added. "She sounds like an interesting woman."

"She seemed nice enough, once I spent a little time with her," Charlie conceded with a wary glance at her brother. She hadn't forgotten the heated conversation they'd had the day after the Halloween party. "She's a little reserved—almost intimidating at first—but I guess that's because she's a scientist with such a serious job."

Her boyfriend, Drew, gave her a look of approval that showed he, too, had given her some advice about Catherine.

"I think it's great that Mike's seeing a scientist," Amy said loyally. "I always thought he needed more of a challenge than those party girls you and Laurie kept introducing him to."

"Weren't you the one who nagged him at Easter about settling down with some nice young woman and starting a family?" Laurie challenged in return. "I'm not sure Dr. Travis is interested in taking time out of her career to raise children."

"And why would she have to choose one or the other?" Gretchen demanded. "I'm raising children and pursuing my career quite successfully, thank you."

Mick spoke up before an all-too-familiar squabble broke out among the four outspoken and opinionated sisters. "Did you do something different to the green beans this year, Alice?" he asked loudly, holding up a forkful to study it. "They don't taste quite the same as usual."

"I brought the green beans, Dad," Charlie— who cooked only when absolutely necessary— said. "I just seasoned them a little differently, that's all. Cut out the fat."

"They taste pretty good," her father conceded. "I kind of miss the ham hock, though."

His daughters immediately began to chide him about eating a more healthy diet. Knowing exactly what had brought about that change of subject, Mike gave his father a grateful look that was returned with a wry smile.

Though she made a point of smiling and nodding, Catherine had no clue what was being said around her as she plowed determinedly through a Thanksgiving dinner she barely tasted. Everyone around her seemed to be in a festive spirit, which made her own somber mood even more difficult to hide.

"Isn't that right, Catherine?" Bill asked from beside her.

She started. "I'm sorry. What did you say?"

The expressions around her told her she had not been doing as good a job as she had hoped of in pretending to be participating. Avoiding Karen's too-perceptive gaze, she made more of an effort to pay attention.

She didn't want to be ungracious. Already she was wondering if she should have canceled— not to accompany Mike, she assured herself, but to stay home alone with her cat and her bruised feelings.

She hadn't heard from Mike since he had stormed out of her apartment. And she had missed him. She was still angry with him, still convinced that he had been a total jerk about her turning down his last-minute invitation to Thanksgiving dinner, but she missed him, anyway. Even more than she would have expected.

It was probably over between them. Mike would move on, going back to his more-fun friends. It was likely that he would find some young, adoring woman who wouldn't ask him questions he didn't want to answer, or challenge him to pursue dreams he seemed hesitant to acknowledge. Maybe his sister's perky blond friend, she thought, trying very hard not to be catty. Knowing she failed.

As for herself, she had her work and her friends. Her cat. Her parents, who would be back in the country in only a few weeks. A good life.

Bill was making it plain that he was still open to seeing her, if she was interested. Wasn't that what she had wished for only a few months earlier? Someone to share her life with? Someone who understood her work and her obligations, who had enough in common with her to form a solid, mutually supportive partnership.

Had she been asked to define her ideal match back then, she would have described someone very much like Bill. And yet, as she sat here beside him now, she felt nothing except admiration and general liking. He was an attractive man, but she had no interest at all in getting any closer to him.

There was more to romantic chemistry than similar careers and educational backgrounds, she understood now. She had never really cared what Mike did for a living—but she did insist on being treated with respect in return.

If Mike couldn't understand that, then he was as wrong for her as Bill was.

"So what happened between you and Catherine, anyway?" Bob asked as he lounged on Mike's rather battered hand-me-down couch with a football game playing on the TV in front of them.

Mike glared at the screen, though his scowl had nothing to do with the fumble that had just taken place there. "It just didn't work out."

"She dumped you, huh?" Bob spoke as if there could be no other logical explanation.

"She didn't dump me. We just split up, that's all."

"I liked her, you know. When you said you were seeing a scientist-professor type, I expected her to be all snooty and dull, but she wasn't like that. I mean, yeah, she needs to learn how to relax a little, but she's not a snob. And she has a sense of humor, which is more than I can say for some good-looking women like that. I know me and Brandon gave you a hard time about being all involved with her and neglecting us and all, but I could sure understand what you saw in her."

Mike grunted and took a swig of the canned soda in his hand, unable to think of anything to say. Almost two weeks after Thanksgiving, his emotions were still too raw to discuss what had gone wrong between himself and Catherine with any degree of objectivity.

"I guess she got tired of you always being late and stuff, huh?"

Mike winced, remembering her last pointed remark to him. "Why do you keep trying to put it all on me?" he complained to his friend—who should be on his side, damn it.

"Just trying to understand what happened. I hate to see you moping around the way you have been the past few days. Maybe we can figure out what went wrong so you can fix it."

"Give it up, Bob. It's over. I think she's seeing someone else, anyway. A doctor. A cardiologist.

Way more in her league than I ever was." Picturing Catherine with Bill James had been like acid in his gut ever since Thanksgiving, keeping him awake at night and interfering with his concentration during the days.

At least he had been spared actually seeing them together. If Bill had been to Catherine's apartment, Mike hadn't seen him. Of course, he'd been assiduously avoiding going anywhere near her apartment except when absolutely necessary for his work. And maybe she had been avoiding him just as determinedly, because he hadn't even caught a glimpse of her in the past couple of weeks.

He missed her. He even missed her cat, darn it. How incredibly stupid had he been to allow himself to fall in love with a woman who had been destined from the beginning to break his heart?

"Oh, man, I'm sorry to hear that. I thought the two of you made a great couple. I didn't think she really cared about the job thing."

"She said she didn't. But when it came to

spending Thanksgiving with me or with the doctor, she chose him," Mike confided bitterly, still stinging over her rejection.

"No kidding? You didn't tell me that before. You mean she canceled your Thanksgiving plans to go out with him? I can't believe it."

"Well, no, that isn't exactly what happened. I mean, I asked her, but she had already accepted an invitation from another friend who had also invited the doctor to dinner. An obvious fix-up, and Catherine had to know it."

"Oh. So, when did you ask her?"

Mike cleared his throat. "The Sunday before Thanksgiving."

After a heavy pause, Bob said slowly, "You waited until four days before Thanksgiving to ask her and then you were pissed off because she already had other plans?"

Scowling, Mike crossed his arms over his chest. "It wasn't exactly like that," he said, even though something inside him insisted it was exactly like that. "I didn't know if I should ask her. I mean, spending holidays with a guy's family is a big deal. Some women get real nervous about that sort of thing. I wasn't sure Catherine and I had reached that point, and I didn't want to scare her off. But we'd had a great weekend, and it seemed like the right time, so…"

Wincing at the inadequacy of his own argument, he let his words trail off.

Bob's silence said a great deal.

"Okay, so it was probably all my fault," Mike erupted angrily, throwing his hands in the air in frustration. "I didn't deserve her. She was too good for me. What else do you want me to say?"

"Sounds like you're the only one who believed all that garbage," Bob observed with uncharacteristic perception. "Maybe you sabotaged it because you wanted to be the one to get out first, before she dumped you."

"I did not—" Mike stopped to draw a deep breath. "I'm not going to fight with you about this. This conversation is closed."

Bob shrugged. "Whatever, dude. Got any more chips?"

Even as he stalked into the kitchen to retrieve

another bag of chips, Mike knew he would be nagged by the echo of Bob's comments for hours to come.

Chapter Sixteen

"Norman, come down from there *now!*" Catherine had tried pleading, cajoling and reasoning, and she was finally resorting to demanding.

She had no more luck with that tactic. Norman remained exactly where he had been for the past twenty minutes. On top of the roof of her apartment building.

Standing on the tiny balcony outside her living room, she craned her neck to gaze up at him with a mixture of fear and exasperation. She was stunned that he was up there, and still not exactly sure how it had happened. She didn't have a clue how she was going to get him down if he refused to cooperate.

A cold December wind blew around her, and she shivered in her thin sweater. She wasn't wearing her coat, but she didn't want to take her eyes off Norman long enough to go inside for it. It was going to be dark soon—it was already dusk—and she wanted him safely back inside her apartment. The problem was, he didn't seem to be in any hurry to get there.

"Norman, please," she said, holding up her arms. "Come inside. I have salmon treats. Yum."

Staring inscrutably back down at her, he tucked his tail around his feet and sat without moving.

She pushed her hands through her hair, growing desperate. Should she call the fire department? The rental office? Who was she supposed to turn to in a situation like this?

"Catherine? Is everything okay up there?"

She looked over the balcony railing with a surge of relief. "Mike?"

He stood on the sidewalk beneath her, toolbox in hand, a heavily lined denim jacket protecting him from the wind. A frown of bewilderment creased his face. "What are you doing? Is everything okay?"

"It's Norman," she said, pointing upward. "He's on the roof."

"He's *what?*"

"He's on the roof," she called back down, aware of a few people in the parking lot turning to stare at her. "I can't get him down. And I'm afraid he—"

"I'm coming up. Stay where you are. Don't lose sight of him. I'll let myself in."

Gratefully, she turned back to her stubborn cat. "Did you hear that, Norman? Mike's coming. You like Mike, remember?"

Norman meowed, but he stayed where he was.

Moments later, Mike stepped onto the balcony. Except for a couple of glimpses of him across the apartment compound, brief incidents that had left her aching, this was the first time she had seen him since their breakup. Even as worried as she was about Norman, she couldn't completely ignore the quiver that ran through her when Mike came to a stop within a few inches of her.

"What happened?" he asked, staring up at Norman. "How did he get up there?"

"I opened the balcony door to bring out this Christmas wreath," she said, pointing to a festive decoration at her feet. "One of the grad students in my department made it for me and I thought it would be pretty hanging from the railing with this big, red bow."

Totally irrelevant to his question, she realized abruptly. Between her concern for Norman and her nervousness at being with Mike again, she was reduced to babbling. "Anyway, the minute I opened the door, Norman streaked past me, jumped up on the railing, then onto that branch and on the roof. He's been there ever since, just staring at me."

Mike looked from the door to the railing to the low branch of the oak tree next to her apartment, mentally following the cat's path. "How long has he been up there?"

"I don't know. Twenty, twenty-five minutes. I've tried everything I know to get him down."

She had been unable to prevent a slight tremor from entering her voice, nor a shiver from passing through her when another cold breeze swirled around them.

Mike stripped off his coat and wrapped it around her shoulders. "Hold this for me. I'm going up after him."

"How are you—"

But Mike was already boosting himself onto the railing, one hand on the wall to brace himself. Now Catherine was frightened all over again. "Mike, be careful. You could fall."

"I'm being careful." Balanced precariously on the three-inch-wide metal railing, he stretched out a hand toward the cat.

"Come on, Norman," he said gently. "Don't make me climb up there to get you, guy. We'd probably end up breaking both our necks."

Norman meowed, twitched his tail and studied Mike's outstretched hand. After what seemed to Catherine like an agonizingly long time, the cat rose, padded easily across the shingles, walked up Mike's arm and perched on his shoulder. He stayed there while Mike climbed carefully down from the railing, with a little help from Catherine.

Back on solid concrete again, Mike reached up to peel Norman's claws out of his gray sweatshirt. "Maybe you'd better take him inside before he decides to go off adventuring again."

Catherine gathered Norman to her gratefully. "Thank you so much. I didn't know how I was going to—"

"Just take him in," Mike interrupted gently. "I'll hang your wreath while I'm out here."

"Oh, you don't have to—" But once again he acted despite her protest, reaching down to pick up the wreath and turning toward the railing with it.

Knowing when retreat was called for, Catherine carried her pet into the safety of the apartment, scolding him gently as she did so.

"What on earth got into you, Norman? Don't you know you could have been hurt? Why is it that you only seem to make these reckless escapes when Mike is around? It makes me look like a very careless pet owner, I can assure you."

Norman made a funny sound that almost resembled a snort of amusement. She looked at him suspiciously. If she didn't know better, she would swear that cat understood every word she said.

The glass door opened and Mike entered, closing it behind him. His hair was wind tossed and his cheeks were cold reddened. Only then did she realize that she was still wearing his coat.

Setting Norman down hastily, she slipped out of the coat and held it out to Mike. "Thank you. For everything. I don't know what I would have done if you hadn't come along."

"He probably would have come down, anyway. He was just waiting until it looked like his idea."

She couldn't smile in response to his quip. For one thing, she was still shaken over Norman's stunt. For another...Mike was in her living room again. And having him here brought back all the pain and longing that had been tormenting her since he had stormed out after their quarrel.

Suddenly self-conscious, she pushed her hands into the pockets of the gray wool slacks she wore with a mint-green sweater set. She'd had a faculty meeting at work that day, so she'd dressed a bit more nicely than usual. "Um, how are things going with you?"

He shrugged, his expression suddenly hard to read. "Okay, I guess. I finished my classes. Passed them both."

"Congratulations." She didn't ask if he had registered for the next semester, though she wanted to. It was no longer any of her business—if it ever had been.

Mike glanced around the room, avoiding her gaze. "Is there anything else you need while I'm here? Any maintenance problems?"

"No," she said in little more than a whisper. "Nothing's broken."

Except her heart, of course. And that was something he had shattered, himself.

Mike nodded and moved toward his door, his

coat draped over one arm. She watched as he placed a hand on the doorknob and she braced herself to watch him walk out again.

Instead he just stood there, staring at the door.

"Mike?" she said after a moment. "Is there something else you want to say?"

"Yeah," he said without turning around. "But I don't know exactly how to begin."

Moistening her lips, she said, "Just say it."

"It's not that easy to admit to being a total ass. My behavior was inexcusable, and I owe you an apology."

A huge lump formed in her throat, forcing her to swallow hard. "You said some very hurtful things to me that night."

"I know. You didn't deserve them."

"I didn't go to Karen's because of Bill. I wasn't seeing him then and I haven't seen him since except in passing at the hospital."

Still without looking at her, he muttered, "I wouldn't blame you if you were. He seemed like a decent guy. And I was a jerk."

Crossing her arms tightly in front of her, she

studied the back of his head. "We both lost our tempers, I guess."

"I know. I was jealous. I guess that's obvious. I didn't think I could compete with a guy like that, and I didn't want you to spend the day with him, comparing us."

"There was never a competition," she said sadly. "I've asked you to stop doing that. Comparing yourself to my other friends. It's pointless. And it's meaningless, since it's something I would never do myself."

"Bob said it was because I never felt good enough for you. He said I was trying to sabotage the relationship before you could dump me and hurt me."

"*Bob* said that?" she asked, startled.

He nodded. "Sometimes he makes more sense than you would expect from him."

There was another tense pause while she thought about Bob's words. And then Mike said, "I've missed you, Catherine. Is there any chance we could try again?"

She couldn't count the number of nights she

had lain awake, fantasizing about hearing him saying those very words. In those scenarios, she had always thrown herself into his arms and assured him that she would love to try again. And that they would make it work this time.

So, it was with great regret that she said, "I don't think that's a very good idea, Mike. I honestly can't see that anything has really changed at all."

His shoulders seemed to sag just a little. "I thought you might say that."

"And that's the biggest problem between us," she whispered. "You still don't trust me. And without trust, there can be nothing else."

She simply couldn't get any more deeply involved with a man who was still convinced that they were destined to fail. It had hurt her so badly when they had broken up before. She couldn't risk going through that—or worse—again.

"I trust you," he insisted. And then he completely negated the statement, in her opinion, by adding, "Would it make any difference if I said I would register for classes next semester?"

He still didn't get it. He still thought he had to prove something to her in order to impress her. He was still selling himself short, and in the process he was doing the same to her.

"I hope you do register for classes, if that's what you want to do. I hope you will pursue your dreams, whatever they are. For your sake, not for anyone else's, including mine. But, no, it doesn't make any difference as far as we are concerned."

She had never cared from the start whether he had a degree. She had fallen for the man he was, not for what he could become. But he still thought she was no different from that woman who had hurt his feelings at his high school reunion. The one who thought herself too good to date a maintenance man.

How could she and Mike ever have a relationship of any sort when he didn't even know her?

He still hadn't looked at her. Maybe he couldn't. He turned the doorknob. "Take care of yourself, Catherine."

"You, too," she choked out.

Norman meowed. Mike hesitated only a moment before letting himself out.

There was no anger in the tears Catherine shed this time. Only deep, painful grief.

Christmas came and went quietly, and somehow Catherine survived the holidays, despite her disinclination to celebrate that year. She hoped she did a credible job of disguising her pain, though she doubted that she fooled Karen or Julia. At least Julia had the compassion not to say I told you so.

Mike quit his job at the apartment complex. The first Catherine knew of it was when she stopped by the office to pay her rent for January and Lucille mentioned it in passing.

"It was a real shame, too," the apartment manager said regretfully. "He was the best we ever had here. Not that I really expected him to stay, a young, good-looking guy like that."

"Does he, um, still live here in the complex?" Catherine had asked, struggling to hide her feelings.

"No. He moved out last weekend. Darn shame," Lucille said again.

After that, Catherine threw herself into her work with a vengeance, spending even longer hours than usual in the lab and in her office. She found herself slipping into her old routines, wearing her same old clothes, coming home to sit with Norman and read her science papers in the evenings.

She couldn't say she never thought of Mike, but she took some pride in reducing those thoughts to no more than once or twice an hour. She had spent a lot of time replaying their time together, asking herself what had gone wrong. She had come to the conclusion that both she and Mike had been at fault.

She had blamed him at first for having such a defeatist attitude toward their relationship, but now she could see that she had done the same thing. She had simply assumed from the start that what they had couldn't last.

It had been a self-fulfilling prediction, she realized now. One a scientist should know better than to make without compelling evidence. But the experiment had failed, for whatever reason, and she still wasn't sure exactly what she had learned as a result.

She wished she knew what he was doing now. Where he was working. Whether he was happy. And she wondered if she would ever stop missing him.

She was pushing a grocery cart out of a local supermarket on a sunny afternoon in February when she heard a familiar voice speak her name. "Hey, Catherine."

Turning, she saw Bob Sharp pushing a delivery cart toward the store entrance, dressed in a blue work uniform, his bright red hair flowing from beneath a blue cap emblazoned with his company's name. A pang went through her at the reminder of Mike. The two months that had passed since she had last seen him had not lessened the ache that accompanied every thought of him.

"Hello, Bob. How are you?" she asked as she

moved her cart out of the way of patrons on their way in and out of the supermarket.

"If I was any better, I wouldn't be able to stand myself."

His cocky answer made her smile. "I'm glad to hear that. It's really good to see you again."

He winked at her. "You, too, Dr. Gorgeous. How's that hot, single lawyer friend of yours? Did you ever tell her about the fantastic, fun guy you found for her?"

She shook her head, her chin brushing against the warm green cashmere scarf she wore with a quilted ski jacket to protect her from the winter chill. "The truth is, she just doesn't deserve you, Bob."

He heaved a sigh. "Though that could go either way, I'll take it as a compliment."

"You should. It was meant as one."

He reached out to chuck her chin with his knuckles. "Thanks, Doc. So, how've you been? Still seeing that cardiologist?"

"I was never seeing a cardiologist," she replied tartly. "That was just an unfounded rumor."

His red eyebrows rose in surprise. "Is that right?"

"Yes."

"Mike's an idiot."

Surprisingly, her lips twitched with a near smile. After a moment she asked, "How is he?"

"I don't see him much," Bob replied with a shrug. "He's real busy being a full-time student and all. He's got a part-time job working for the university. Doing some odd jobs around campus for extra cash."

"He's going to school full-time?"

Bob nodded. "He sort of made the decision at the last minute, almost too late to enroll for the semester. I think it was sometime during Christmas. He'd been moping around for days, and then he just jumped into this plan. He's been going like a windup bunny ever since, hardly ever giving himself a chance to breathe, as far as I can tell."

Her fingers tightened almost painfully around the handle of her shopping cart. "Do you know if he's declared a major?"

Bob grinned. "You might not believe it. It's education. He says he wants to be a teacher. When I think back about what he was like in school, and remember what a trial he was to all his own teachers, I can't help but laugh."

But Catherine wasn't laughing. In fact, she was having a hard time not bursting into tears. "I think it's great," she said, forcing out the words.

Bob's grin faded as he searched her face. "Hey, you want me to give him a message from you next time I talk to him?"

There were so many messages she would have liked to send. I'm proud of you. I miss you. I'm still in love with you. But all she said was, "Just give him my best."

"Catherine—"

"Gosh, I'd better get going. I have frozen things melting in my cart as we stand here." It was a patently flimsy excuse, since the temperature was hardly warm enough to melt anything for some time yet. But she couldn't stand there any longer, trying to keep her raw feelings hidden. "Goodbye, Bob. It was great to see you."

He didn't try to detain her. But she knew he watched her closely as she hurried away.

Hands in the pockets of his jeans, Mike looked up at the window above his head, smiling a little when he saw a black-and-white head peering back down at him from the windowsill inside. Funny how much he had missed that sight in the past months.

The last time he'd stood here it had been cold, and a Christmas wreath had hung from a big red bow on the balcony above him. Bundled into a coat against the bleak December day, he had stood in this very spot for a long time, gazing up at Norman as they had silently said their goodbyes before Mike walked away for the last time. Of course he had known Norman hadn't really been aware that it was goodbye, but Mike had liked carrying that fantasy away with him when he'd climbed into his loaded truck and driven away from the apartments that had been his home for such a short time.

Now Norman sat in the very same place, as though he hadn't moved in the meantime, even though May flowers bloomed around the complex and Mike wore a short-sleeved shirt with his jeans and sneakers. It had been gray and cloudy that day; now the sky was a brilliant blue dotted with only a few fluffy white cotton-candy puffs. So many things were different—not the least of which was Mike, himself.

He knew Catherine was home, because her car was in its usual space. What he didn't know was how she would react at finding him at her door. Half tempted to turn around and climb back into his truck, he wondered where he was going to find the nerve to climb those stairs and find out.

Catherine moved to answer her door, still distracted by an article she had been reading, when someone rang the bell. It was with only idle curiosity that she checked the peephole to see who stood on the other side.

The scientific journal fell unnoticed to her

feet when she saw who it was. She pressed a hand to her chest, where her heart was suddenly pounding, and stared at the doorknob, trying to remember how to use it.

Norman butted against her leg, meowing with what sounded like impatience for her to open the door. Spurred into action, she reached out and opened the door. "Mike?"

He looked exactly as he had the first time she had seen him, though he wasn't wearing the ID badge this time. His dark-blond hair was still a little shaggy and wind tossed, and his eyes were as vividly blue as ever. He still looked like someone who should be cavorting on a beach somewhere, or posing for ads for casual men's wear.

He was still the most attractive man Catherine could ever imagine meeting.

"Bob was only partially right," he said, for all the world as if only moments had passed since they had last spoken. "It wasn't our relationship I was trying to sabotage. It was everything it represented."

She had no clue what she was supposed to say in response to that. Except… "Um, would you like to come in?"

He stepped inside and closed the door behind him, but he shook his head when she automatically waved him to a seat. "No, I need to say this," he said, looking as though he had rehearsed a speech and wanted to get it all out before he forgot any of it. "Even if this is the last time we see each other, you deserve to know what I finally figured out about myself since we split."

"And what is that?" she asked, studying him curiously, her racing pulse beginning to slow, but not by much.

"I wasn't afraid of competing with your friends," he admitted. "I was afraid of becoming one of them. Grown up. Responsible. Tied down. I liked not being committed to anything, not even to the classes I was taking just to appease other people. I didn't have to care about my grades because I wasn't really trying to earn a degree, anyway. I didn't have to worry too much about my responsibilities to my job, because it was one I could walk away from at any time. And I figured I didn't have to work too hard at our relationship because it wasn't going to last, anyway. And there was a part of me that liked it that way."

He paused to draw a breath, then added, "Those things I said about not having the right education or not fitting in with your friends—those were just excuses I told myself. I knew they weren't insurmountable obstacles between us, but it was easier to pretend that they were. Like I said, they were excuses for me to walk away."

The words hurt. But as he had said, she deserved to hear them. "And have you come here today to tell me you've changed your attitude about those things?"

He shook his head and pulled a folded sheet of paper out of the pocket of his shirt. "I came to show you this."

She took the crumpled sheet from him curiously, unfolding it after an encouraging nod from him. It was a grade sheet, she saw immediately. He had taken four classes, a total of thirteen credit hours. He had two As—one in the four-hour class—and two Bs.

"This is a very good transcript," she said slowly, looking up at his face again. "Why did you want me to see it?"

"You're a scientist. You need proof," he said lightly, though his eyes were entirely serious. "That's why I made myself wait this long to come to you, even though I knew I was taking a risk that you'd have moved on. Forgotten all about me."

Forget about him? Fat chance, she thought, though she remained quiet as he continued speaking.

"It took commitment to get those grades. I had to work my butt off. And I did it for me, not for you. Not for anyone else. It took commitment to sign the papers for student loans I'm going to have to pay back eventually. I knew when I signed them that I couldn't just walk away this time. Scared the socks off me, but I signed them. For my sake."

She had to speak up then. "I never cared whether you had a degree."

He nodded. "I know. You really didn't care that I was a maintenance worker. I was the one who wasn't any more committed to that job than I was to my classes. I liked the job well enough, but when I looked ahead long-term, I knew it wasn't what I really wanted to do. It wasn't the commitment I wanted to make. Bob helped me understand that, too."

"What did he say?"

"It wasn't what he said. I just took a good look at him. That delivery job? He loves it. He sticks with it because it's exactly what he wants to be doing. He likes being outside, likes being mobile, likes gabbing with all the people he encounters during the day. He says maybe someday he'll aim for a promotion, maybe a district supervisor in the same field, but in the meantime, he's genuinely happy with his job. He could go into a group of your friends with his head held high and genuine pride in his work because he chose that job for the right reasons.

I didn't have that same satisfaction in my own job, which I chose mostly because it didn't require much of me."

"And yet you did it very well," she pointed out, hating to hear him criticize himself quite so harshly.

He nodded. "Yeah. Even when I was trying to convince myself I wasn't the responsible and committed type, I took pride in my work. That's one of the things that convinced me that maybe I wasn't a hopeless cause, after all."

"I never thought you were hopeless," she murmured.

"No," he said quietly. "You always said you supported me no matter what I wanted to do. Whether it was maintenance work, or teaching and coaching, you didn't really seem to care. All you ever asked for from me was honesty. And I wasn't giving you that. That's what you were trying to tell me."

She nodded. For the first time since he had shown up at her door, she allowed herself a glimmer of hope.

"It wouldn't be easy being involved with a debt-ridden college student. Your friends who are further along in their careers would think you were lowering yourself, maybe. Even though they were perfectly nice to me when I did spend an evening with them," he added quickly. "Well, except for Julia, maybe, but I could win her over with time."

"I wouldn't be surprised if you could," she murmured, fighting a sudden, inappropriate urge to smile.

"So, here's the thing," Mike said after another deep breath, looking as though he were launching back into the prepared speech. "I don't need your money—I have loans and a part-time job to cover my education. I don't need to be tutored—I made those grades on my own. What I need is someone to be by my side—on my side—as I work toward my goals."

He held up a hand when she started to speak. "I haven't told you what I have to offer in return," he reminded her. "I'm an entertaining guy. I know how to help a serious workaholic relax and have fun every once in a while. I'm handy around the house. I have a good track record of rescuing runaway cats. I've got some terrific little nieces and nephews I'd be happy to share with an aspiring book-and-chemistry-set-giving aunt. I've got a heart filled with love. I've spent the past six months learning how to make commitments. I'm prepared to make one to you, as soon as you're ready to accept it. And I can be patient. I'll give you as much time as you want, to decide if you're willing to take another risk on me."

He had said so much, given her so many things to think about—but only one statement stood out to her. Had he really said he loved her?

Looking increasingly anxious as she continued to remain silent, Mike asked, "Is it no use, Catherine? Do you want me to go?"

Norman butted her leg again, meowing rather loudly.

She moistened her lips. "You've been so busy blaming yourself for everything that went wrong that you haven't given me a chance to tell you how I contributed to the sabotage."

He shook his head, looking suddenly stubborn. "You didn't do anything wrong. I was the one who—"

"My turn," she broke in. "Hear me out. You said you were using the excuse that you weren't good enough for me. I had the same fears, you know. I was protecting myself, predicting the worst, refusing to fight for us for similar reasons."

"How could you possibly think you weren't good enough for me?"

"It wasn't like that, exactly. But I was afraid that maybe I wasn't interesting enough to hold your attention. Your other friends seemed so much younger and zanier and more fun. Prettier, wittier, more impulsive. For all I knew, you would grow bored with dating a boring scientist with staid, quiet friends. So maybe *I* wanted to be the one to end it first, before I got hurt."

"That's the most ridiculous thing I've ever heard," he said, staring at her as if she had suddenly started speaking in a foreign language.

"No more ridiculous than you thinking I

would dump you because I was embarrassed about your job," she answered tartly.

"How could you possibly think I would get bored with you? I'm in love with you. I have been since almost the beginning, and that hasn't changed even during all the time we've been apart."

"And how could you think I really cared if you had a degree or what uniform you wore to your job?" she returned. "I'm in love with *you*, not your résumé."

He went very still. Realizing exactly what she had just said, she did the same. They stood there for a long time, simply staring at each other. And then Mike reached out for her.

Norman retreated in satisfaction as Catherine melted into Mike's arms.

"You were gone for so long," she sighed a while later as he loomed over her in her bed.

He cupped her face between his hands and smiled ruefully down at her. "I had a lot of growing up to do."

"I suppose we both did," she replied, tugging

him down to her. Apparently, they had both learned some valuable lessons during the past months, Catherine thought, eagerly welcoming him home. "But you're back now."

"I'm back now," he repeated against her lips. "And this time I'm here to stay."

* * * * *